Remember when a
good love story made you feel
like holding hands?

Harlequin presents

# LEOPARD
## in the
# SNOW
...*a love story*

D1111958

Coming soon to a theater near you!

OTHER
*Harlequin Romances*
by ISOBEL CHACE

# Second Best Wife

by

## ISOBEL CHACE

**Harlequin Books**

TORONTO • LONDON • NEW YORK • AMSTERDAM • SYDNEY

Original hardcover edition published in 1978
by Mills & Boon Limited

ISBN 0-373-02176-3

Harlequin edition published June 1978

PRINTED IN U.S.A.

# CHAPTER ONE

Georgina had first met the redoubtable William Ayres when she was ten years old. She had disliked him on sight, mostly because at fifteen he hadn't looked like a boy at all but a fully grown man. Worse still, he had made his reputation locally as a wit at her expense and she would never, never forgive him for that, not if she lived to be a hundred and one.

It had been at a village children's party which, as far as she was concerned, had begun badly and had got steadily worse as the afternoon had gone on, until that brief, devastating moment when William had made her the laughing-stock of the whole community. Georgina had been told to look after her nine-year-old sister, as she always was, and had been taking the duty as seriously as she always did. This had largely consisted of defending Jennifer from the village bully, a boy named Duncan Radcliffe. She had been remarkably successful too, for her flair for organisation and her practical way of going about things in general had already been in evidence at that tender age. She had only turned her back once in two hours, but it had been enough for Duncan to pull Jennifer's skinny plaits and twist her arms, and then, of course, half a dozen adults had stood between him and the revenge Georgina would have meted out to him then and there.

So Georgina had bided her time. She had waited for the inevitable game of Postman's Knock—a game she thought remarkably silly at the best of times—and had waited her turn to choose Duncan as her victim. She had even pretended to kiss him, but at the last moment she had drawn back her fist and had hit him, hard, on the nose. And

Duncan had cried and she had been *glad* he had cried.

And then it was that William, bored stiff by the doings of his juniors, had opened his mouth and drawled,

'*Georgie Porgie, pudding and pie, Kissed the boys and made them cry!*

A roar of laughter had greeted this sally, the more so for Georgina was a solid little girl who had not yet fined down into the slim, well-made woman she was now. The nursery rhyme had followed her wherever she went. Even Jennifer had begun to shorten her name to Georgie, accompanied by a silly giggle that never failed to make the discomfited Georgina see red. One day, she had vowed to herself, *one day* she would teach William Ayres a lesson he would never forget and everyone would laugh at *him* as they had laughed at her!

Now, thirteen years later, the instrument of his punishment had fallen into her hands and the unassuaged bitterness of years rose in her throat, blinding her to the difficulties that still lay ahead of her. It had not taken her very long to discover that William disliked her almost as much as she disliked him. She had thought it a pity that that dislike hadn't been extended to Jennifer as well, but her sister had blossomed into a frail, gentle young woman, unable to make up her mind about anything, but so sweet-natured that nobody minded her ineffectual ways. As far as boys were concerned she was a regular honeypot, which Georgina was not. Perhaps to make up for her sister's lack of character and push, Georgina had a practical streak that verged on the managing and a defensive attitude to life that made her as prickly as a hedgehog and not sweet at all.

It had been last year that William had asked Jennifer to marry him, and Jennifer, unwilling as ever to hurt him by telling him that she wanted to marry someone quite different, had blurted out her consent and had then run to Georgina to get her out of it, just as she always had.

Georgina's moment of triumph had been sweet. She had

tasted it on her tongue and had found it good. Not normally vindictive, she had known she was going to enjoy telling him of her sister's defection. Her moment of complete, devastating revenge had come!

Georgina stared at herself in the looking-glass, pulling a face at the strongly defined features that stared back at her. Where Jennifer was so fair as to be almost wholly pink and white, broken up only by the pale blue of her eyes, Georgina's hair was black, her eyes the grey-green of a stormy sea, and her face as tanned as any gypsy's—and she had known a few for, once upon a time, they had been allowed to camp quite close to the village where she had been brought up. They never came now, for the police had long ago been given orders to move them on as fast as they had arrived in the district and, as far as Georgina knew, she was the only person who missed them.

She sighed, wishing her chin was a little less square and her mouth a little less firm, even if it did kick up at the corners when she smiled. Her father had once told her she had a passionate mouth, but he had been laughing when he had said it and she had known in her heart of hearts that he, too, secretly preferred the rosebud curves to Jennifer's lips, often left slightly open to accommodate her slightly prominent teeth and to relieve her neat but not very practical nose.

It was no wonder that William had fallen for Jennifer, Georgina thought. There was no danger of Jennifer challenging any of the dictates he had handed out to them both during the years of their adolescence. It had always been she, Georgina, who had fallen foul of the temper which she had known from the start he possessed and which she had taken some pleasure in provoking whenever she could, frightened as she had been at times of the cold rage that had possessed him, swamping his normally excellent judgement, and closing his mind completely to the reasoned practicalities she had deliberately offered him, fanning the flames of their mutual dislike.

But Jennifer had not fallen for William. Georgina had feared she would, for Jennifer liked what she called 'strong' people, but in the end she had chosen someone almost as gentle and undefined as herself, a man Georgina had despised from the first moment she had set eyes on him. Imagine her astonishment, therefore, when Jennifer had introduced him as the grown-up version of that juvenile bully, Duncan Radcliffe, of whom she had been so afraid when they had been respectively nine and ten years old.

'*You're* Duncan Radcliffe?' Georgina had accosted him in accusing tones. 'You can't be! Duncan was a beast!'

Duncan had smiled sweetly back at her. 'People ignored me,' he had explained diffidently. 'I was always trying to get them to listen and they never did. *You* always made me cry, I remember. I was scared stiff of you. Whenever I managed to say a single word to Jennifer you would come up and bash me.'

'You bullied her!'

And Jennifer had gone a delicious pink and had said, 'Yes, but I liked it, Georgie. He never hurt me as you did. I told you so at the time, but you were too busy quarrelling with William to pay any attention to anyone else.' She had giggled suddenly. 'Duncan and I thought it awfully clever of him to bring out that funny rhyme at that party! We laughed about it for months afterwards!'

Months? It had been *years* before Georgina had heard the last of that particular nursery rhyme, years in which she had seen to it that even if nobody had forgotten it, just as she had never been able to forget the burning humiliation of that moment, they never dared to repeat it any more in her hearing. It had cost her dear, but she had come out on top in the end. Even Jennifer had received a black eye when she had repeated the offending verse in an incautious moment.

Georgina had given them both a bewildered look. 'But

what about all the times he pulled your hair and twisted your arms?' she had asked Jennifer.

They had both of them smiled at that. 'You wouldn't understand, Georgie,' they had said together. 'It only meant that we liked each other.'

Georgina didn't understand now, but she had understood at once when they had, both of them, shuffled their feet and looked slightly pathetic and had asked her if she would mind breaking the news to William.

Georgina's eye had gleamed with a long-awaited triumph. 'That will be a pleasure,' she had said. And she had meant it, every word of it.

But walking along the short distance between the Perry household and the much grander residence where William Ayres' parents lived, she began to wonder if it was really going to be the kind of revenge she would enjoy after all. She had never felt sorry for William before and it would ruin everything if she were to feel any sympathy for him now. He hadn't felt sorry for *her* when he had made her the butt of the whole village's somewhat simple brand of humour!

Georgina opened the gate and walked into the pleasant garden that surrounded the rose-pink brick building that she had always thought wasted on anyone as undiscerning as William. She stood for a moment, running her eyes over its familiar features with a hunger she would have spurned had she been aware of it. The Perry house where she lived was as bleak and bald as this one was gracious and welcoming.

'Well, if it isn't Georgie Porgie,' William's voice broke into her thoughts, making the hairs prickle on her neck with hatred for him. 'What's brought you into the lion's den?'

'Certainly not your charm, William Ayres,' she snapped back at him. 'I was wondering how you could have lived in such surroundings all these years and yet be so uncharming.' She wanted to tell him that he was more like a scorpion than a lion, but her innate honesty of mind forbade the attack. He did look remarkably like a lion, with lion-coloured shaggy hair and eyes the colour sometimes of warm toffee and sometimes of sunburned grass.

'What do you want?' he asked her wearily.

It was so unusual for William to be anything but terse and faintly taunting when he spoke to her that she was thrown off balance by the dullness of his tone of voice.

'I'd hardly have come for my own pleasure,' she retorted tartly.

He leaned on the spade he had been wielding, looking her up and down. 'Give it a rest, Georgie. I could see from the cut of your jib the moment you opened the gate that you'd come to give me a set-down. Why don't you get it over with?'

She narrowed her eyes, resenting the intimate way he was looking at her. He didn't see her as a desirable female, so he shouldn't look at her as if he did. 'It's too good to hurry,' she murmured, forcing a smile. 'Much too good to hurry!'

He picked up the spade and dropped it into the ground. The metal cut through the hard ground as easily as a hot knife through butter. Unaccountably, Georgina took a step backwards, knowing that that was what he'd like to do to her and feeling suddenly unsure of herself.

'Well?' he said.

'It isn't really good,' she contradicted herself. She took a deep breath, averting her eyes from the mockery in his. 'Oh dear, I wish she'd told you herself now, but Jennifer would just leave you hanging on for ever——'

To her surprise William grinned at her. 'She hasn't your gift for quick surgery,' he agreed. Then he sobered, his mouth settling into a grim line. 'Get on with it, girl! And don't look at me like that! If you think I'm going to bleed all over the garden for your delectation, you're wrong. I wouldn't give you the pleasure of sharing my wounds with you!'

'No, of course not! You've never been vulnerable like the rest of us, have you?' Georgina returned hotly. 'You're as arrogant now as you were *then*! In fact, I think you're worse now, if you want to know.'

'I don't.'

She twisted her fingers together in an agitated movement that betrayed her inner torment. She wasn't enjoying this half as much as she had thought she would. She spent a long moment trying to find the right words to soften the blow she had waited so many years to deal him, but there was no way she could find of wrapping up the unsavoury truth that she had to deliver. Besides, it wasn't her way. She had always looked facts straight in the eye herself and she thought that William did too.

'In ancient times the bearer of bad tidings was often killed for bringing them to the ear of the king,' she said at last.

'Is that why you're nervous? Because you think I might murder you for enjoying sticking pins in me? Not in cold blood, my dear Georgie. Of course there's no saying what I might not do in a rage——'

'Jennifer isn't going to marry you.'

His face hardened. 'On your say-so?'

Georgina opened her eyes wide. 'Why should you think that?'

'Because you've bossed the poor girl about unmercifully ever since I've known you! It was one in the eye for you when we got engaged, wasn't it? Did you have to break it up? Couldn't you have contained your jealousy for your sister just this once?'

Winded, Georgina stuttered a denial which withered on her lips as she read the full depth of his contempt for her in his expression.

'She's going to marry *Duncan*,' she explained.

'Oh, is she? We'll see about that!'

Georgina recovered a little. 'You mean it's all right for you to bully her, but not for me?'

He pulled the spade free of the earth and slammed it down again. 'Heaven give me patience, for you'd try the patience of a saint, Georgina Perry! What made you pick on Duncan of all people?'

'I didn't!'

But she might just as well not have spoken. 'I suppose you found out long ago that he couldn't stand up to you?' he went on nastily. 'Well, I can, Georgie Porgie, and I will. I'll make you rue this day for as long as you live, if it's the last thing I do!'

A shiver of fear ran up Georgina's spine. 'Why me?' she asked almost humbly. 'Why are you always so beastly to me? All right, I wanted to be the one to tell you because— because I've never forgiven you for making everyone laugh at me, and this was the best opportunity I've ever had to hurt you as I was hurt then. But it wasn't anything to do with me that she preferred someone else to you! Anyone would! But you can't take it like a man, can you? Well, I don't believe your silly threats, so there!'

'So there?' There was a trace of cold steel in his amusement. 'How are you going to stop me taking it out on you?'

She faced up to him, swallowing down her momentary fear. 'I'll stay out of your way.'

'Much good that'll do you!'

'It'll be a pleasure!' she told him passionately. 'I don't like you at all—I never have!'

'Because I called your bluff when you made that poor little rabbit of a boy cry? Little girls should be taught early in life to keep their fists to themselves.'

'That was Duncan,' she retorted. 'Duncan Radcliffe. He's the man Jennifer is going to marry instead of you! He was a horrid boy, always pulling Jennie's hair and pinching her.' Her brow wrinkled as she remembered her earlier bewilderment. 'Only Jennie doesn't remember that now.'

'Probably because it never happened outside your imagination. It was most likely the excuse you invented in case anyone asked you why you'd punched the poor little devil. Usually you didn't bother with any excuse. You even took me on once, my girl, and you narrowly missed a good thrashing as a result. If I'd given it to you then, you might not stand in such need of one now!'

She was offended. 'Oh, I *hate* you!' she declared. 'You don't *know* anything about me at all, but you've always pretended you do, and it was never anything to my credit. Jennifer could do no wrong, but I could do no right, could I? Well, for what it's worth, you can do no right as far as I'm concerned either!'

'Pity.'

'And what does that mean?'

He brushed the mud off his fingers, ignoring her. She had a good view of his face in profile and she wondered, briefly, how she would have felt about him if she hadn't learned to hate him so many years before. He had a lot going for him in the way of looks. It was a good, strong face that turned slowly towards her and the eyes that met hers were well-shaped even if they were as cold as a winter's day.

'I'll tell you after I've seen Jennifer and heard her side of this affair. But I warn you, Georgina, if I find you're the cause of things having gone wrong between us, you'll pay for it. If you've messed things up for me, I'll have you instead!'

Her mouth fell open. 'What on earth do you mean by that?'

'I mean,' he said with such restraint that she found herself believing every word of it, 'that you may not be my ideal woman, but you belong to the female sex, more or less, and that's all that's necessary for you to take Jennifer's place and come with me to Sri Lanka. I don't intend to go alone and you, my dear, will hate every moment of it, and that's good enough for me!'

'You're mad!' she gasped.

'If I am, it's because you've driven me round the bend,' he responded with a grunt. 'You've nobody to blame but yourself!'

'If you think——'

He put a hand on her shoulder, his fingers biting into her flesh. 'I don't think, I know. Come along, Georgina, we're going to have a talk with that sister of yours—*both* of us!'

'She's with Duncan,' Georgina protested. 'Can't you see, William, she was afraid to tell you herself? I wish she had! I thought I'd enjoy hurting you——'

'It won't be me who receives the lasting hurt!'

'No, but why hurt me? Why did you have to make them all laugh at me at that party? People went on about it years later, still quoting that stupid rhyme at me. It was so unfair!'

'Life is unfair. Besides, you deserved it and you know you did. A tomboy is one thing, but a termagant is another.'

'I never hit you!'

'Not for lack of trying.' He glanced down meaningly at her clenched fists. 'Are you going to try it now?'

Georgina forgot that discretion is the better part of valour. Her temper flared and she took careful aim, judging her distance nicely. She made exactly the right allowance for him to dodge her blow and caught him fair and square in the eye. At the moment of contact her anger seeped away and she withdrew the guilty fist to cover her mouth, her eyes wide with contrition.

'You dared me to!' she defended herself.

'I can't say I thought you'd do it all the same,' he muttered. He put a hand up to his eye and swore briefly. Georgina was horrified to see that it was already discoloured and more than a little red.

'I'm sorry, but you shouldn't have made me lose my

temper. If we went inside I could bathe it for you.' The colour drained from her face. 'It might look better then before your mother sees it.'

He was startled. 'Does her opinion matter to you?'

Georgina nodded. 'I like her,' she said simply. 'I've always liked her. You're not at all like her.'

'No,' he agreed with feeling. 'I never allowed you to pull the wool over my eyes! Well, now she'll see you as you really are, won't she? As an intemperate, vicious little thug!'

'Because I got the better of you? It was your own fault, only of course you won't admit it! You dared me to hit you, you know you did! I suppose you didn't think I would, that I would slap you or something silly like that, and now you don't like it because it was as good as anything you could do! A fine flush hit! It's made a pretty good mess of your face, let me tell you, and I'm completely unmarked!'

He uttered an exasperated laugh. 'Only because I didn't hit you back!'

'You might not have succeeded,' she pointed out. 'I would have dodged out of the way!'

He turned to face her, reaching out for her and, with a gasp, she rushed out of arm's reach and ran down the garden path towards the gate and the comparative safety of the public highway. William caught her up halfway down the road to her parents' house.

'Have you forgotten I'm coming to see Jennifer?' he asked her sweetly. 'Or did you hope I'd give you time to tell her what to say? Not on your life, my girl! This time you won't shift the responsibility on to anyone else, least of all that long-suffering sister of yours. Jealousy is a very nasty thing and, if you allow it to, it will warp your whole nature. You ought to be grateful to me for making you face up to your motives for doing your best to ruin your sister's life. The only thing I want to know now is did you make

Jennifer agree to marry me in the first place so that you could have your moment of triumph, or are you making her marry Duncan?'

'I suppose you won't believe I've had nothing to do with anything Jennie chooses to do?'

'That would be stretching my credulity too far,' he agreed.

Georgina's eyes stung with tears. 'All right, *ask* Jennifer! I hope you'll feel as much a fool as you'll look when she's told you how wrong you are!'

'*If* she tells me I'm wrong. I've known you both for years, remember, and you've always made Jennifer go your way. You won't do the same to me, so make up your mind to it, Georgina.'

'I wouldn't want to try,' she countered dryly. 'I've never pretended to know everything as you do. I wonder you mix with us lesser beings at all!'

William favoured her with a cold, blank look. 'Nor will that sharp tongue of yours help you. It doesn't cut any ice with me.'

'No,' she said, not without bitterness, 'it takes a pair of bright blue eyes to do that!'

His face flushed with anger. 'Georgina Perry, I'm warning you! Another crack like that and I'll put you across my knee in the middle of the road! It's more than time you learned to control that jealous temperament of yours! Is it Jennifer's fault that men find her more attractive than they do you?'

Georgina formed her lips into a smile. 'Do they?' she tempted him. 'How can you possibly know that?'

'Jennifer——' He broke off, his eyes narrowing.

'Jennifer told you!' Georgina finished for him. 'Such a reliable source of information, I'm told. Still, it's something that you don't pretend to be privy to my love life as well as everything else—it might surprise you, it might even shatter a few illusions, and that would never do, would it?' She was rather proud of the note of mockery she had achieved, knowing he found it as objectionable as he did everything else about her.

'I have no illusions about either you or Jennifer,' he answered her. 'I've known you both far too long.'

'So you have,' she agreed with a light laugh. 'There's none so blind as he who will not see, though. Even the mighty William Ayres isn't always right! And, before you decide it's my vindictive nature that makes me say such a thing, it was your mother who said it first. She said it to comfort *me*. She said when I grew up I wouldn't care what you thought about me——'

'Why do you?' he interrupted her.

She thought of denying that she did, but William was no fool and she knew he would recognise it for the lie it was.

'I don't know,' she said at last. 'Because I'm a fool, I guess. Because you hurt me so badly and I wanted to change your mind about me. *I don't know!*'

'Because you're jealous of Jennifer and you hated anyone to like her better than you. Isn't that the squalid little truth that's driven you on to seek your revenge on me all these years?'

'No, it had nothing to do with Jennifer,' she claimed, but she knew he wasn't even listening. There was an eager look to his face as he marched up the path by her side towards the front door. He had probably forgotten all about her, so intent was he on getting to Jennifer. For the first time she wondered if he were really in love with her sister and she was a little shocked that the question should arise in her mind at all. Why else would he have asked Jennifer to marry him?

Jennifer and Duncan were still sitting in the sitting-room where she had left them. They looked ill at ease when they saw her, glancing at her guiltily out of the corner of their eyes. Georgina felt the old, remembered irritation with her sister that she could never come out into the open and say what she meant. One always had to dig everything out of her bit by bit and, truth to tell, it was seldom worth the trouble when she did finally make her views known.

'Didn't you tell him?' Jennifer asked Georgina now. 'You said you would, Georgie. You said you'd enjoy it!'

'No, I didn't,' Georgina returned calmly.

'It's what you meant, though, you know you did! Why bring him here? I can't possibly see him now. You'll have to get rid of him, darling. He frightens me.'

Georgina turned her head to William who was still waiting in the hall. 'She says you frighten her,' she repeated. 'She'd prefer it if you went away.'

'Or is that what you would prefer?' he demanded. He took a step forward into the doorway, reaching out a hand to Georgina and spinning her out of his way. Unfortunately she lost her balance and collided with the rising Duncan. 'That's right, knock him out too!' William jeered at her.

Jennifer gazed at him with stricken eyes. 'William, your eye! Did Georgie do that?'

'Who else?'

'Oh, how awful of her! I only asked her to——'

'Yes, what did you ask her to say to me?' he asked grimly.

Jennifer fluttered her lashes, glancing briefly at her sister. 'Oh, William, you know I wouldn't have hurt you for anything in the world! I can't help it if I'm easily persuaded, can I? Georgie could always make me say and do anything she wanted me to. I know I ought to stand on my own feet more, but you don't know what it's like when you have a big, overbearing sister like mine! She doesn't mean any harm, only she can't understand that anyone should want to do something else but carry out her commands. You mustn't be angry with her, William dear, or with me either.'

William's mouth set into a dangerous line. 'Meaning that you do want to break off our engagement?'

Jennifer nodded. 'I never wanted to get engaged in the

first place! I wouldn't have done if Georgie hadn't——'

Georgina pulled herself up on to her feet, unable to believe her ears. She felt as though she were drowning and the harder she tried to breathe normally, the worse she felt. She felt dizzy and bells rang in her ears.

'If I hadn't what?' she pressed Jennifer.

'Oh, Georgie, I know you think I'm betraying you to the enemy, but you shouldn't have suggested I did it in the first place. It wasn't a worthy revenge for you to take. You knew I always wanted Duncan and you should never have persuaded me to lead William on. He has every right to be angry with both of us!'

William's hand closed round the nape of Georgina's neck, holding her in a painful grasp. 'I've heard enough!' he declared with a suppressed violence that made Georgina shiver. 'Don't worry, Jennie, I don't blame you for anything. I hope you'll be very happy with your Duncan, though I doubt you will be unless you can find some way of getting Georgie out of your life. I may help you do it! I may very well help you do it!'

Georgina tried to break away from his bruising fingers, but he shook her like a cat does her kitten, reducing her will-power to zero.

'William, please!' she begged him.

'Oh no, you don't, my girl. You're coming with me! For once in your life you're going to pay in full! I'm going to render my account in person and you are going to pay it! Understand?'

Georgina's senses swam. She had seen William in a rage before, but she had never seen him like this, and she was afraid. She was scared silly of what he might do to her and even more scared as to how she might react to whatever he was going to do.

It was then that she knew that she didn't hate William Ayres at all.

# CHAPTER TWO

Georgina could hear the laughter behind her as she struggled against the iron grasp of the man who held her, yanking her out of the room behind him and hauling her through the hall and out the still open front door.

'*Georgie Porgie, pudding and pie, Kissed the boys and made them cry!*'

'You see!' she ground out. '*They've* never forgotten either!'

'How childish can you get?' William asked of no one in particular. 'It must be true for you to mind so much. Is it?'

'*No!*'

'Then why all the fuss? Why try to ruin Jennifer's and my life for such a trivial reason?'

Georgina slowed her pace in an attempt to retrieve some of her dignity which he was doing his best to destroy, jerking her after him as she vainly tried to keep up with his much longer legs.

'I suppose it's useless to say that I didn't?'

'Completely useless.'

They went on in silence with her half-running to keep up with him. 'You're hurting me,' she complained.

'No, I'm not. You're not going to wriggle out of it this time, Georgina, so don't go all soft and feminine on me. It won't work. And *don't* cry! I can't stand whining females!'

Georgina had never whined in her life. 'I'm not crying!'

'Good. Keep it that way. You can cry as much as you like when I've finished telling you what your meddling has got you into. Come to think of it, Meddlesome Matty would have suited you as well as Georgie Porgie. But *this* time *you're* going to pick up the pieces of your own demolition job! I don't see why anyone else should suffer, do you?'

Georgina made another futile effort to ease her hand out of his. 'Just me?' she asked bitterly.

His expression was as bitter as her voice. 'And me. I'll be there, right beside you, and it won't be much fun for me either. But if I can't have Jennifer I'll get what I can out of you——'

'But you don't even like me!'

'No, I don't like you at all, but I'll have the satisfaction of knowing you won't be hurting Jennifer all the time you're with me—and that you'll be hating every moment you find yourself stuck with my society.'

Georgina's legs refused to carry her any further. She came to an abrupt halt, ignoring the searing pain in the muscles of her arm as William tried to force her onward.

'William, don't be daft! I know you're angry at what's happened, but, truly, none of it was my fault. There's no need to behave like a bull chasing a red rag. Sooner or later you're bound to recover yourself and then you'll regret——'

'The regrets will be yours!'

She eyed him cautiously, remembering the results of earlier rages when, blind to everything but the impulse of the moment, William had had every child in the village trembling with fear at what he might do next. His tempers never lasted long, however, and she of all people should have been able to understand them, for she lost her own temper with all the frequency and heat of a redhead. William's rage was never a hot emotion, however, it was cold and deadly and all the worse because he looked so normal all the time he was in the grip of the need to savage anyone who came near him.

'William,' she pleaded, 'remember what happened last time!'

'Tell me about it,' he invited her.

'I wasn't here,' she said uneasily. 'I was away at college. Jennifer told me about it. When I came back you'd moved out of your parents' house—for ever, I hoped!—and Jennifer was in a state that bordered on hysteria because of what you'd said to her. She swore she'd never forgive you!'

'A nice story,' he commented. 'And just what is it I'm supposed to have said to her?'

Georgina pursed up her lips. 'You cast aspersions on her virtue.'

'On *her* virtue? Come off it, Georgie! I never said any such thing. We quarrelled about you as usual and if Jennifer was "in a state", as you put it, it was because she'd just received a letter from you telling her what you would do to her if she got engaged to me. I told her she could leave your reactions to me, but she could never escape from your influence, could she? She didn't believe me and she resented that I had to go away because of my job. How you do twist everything to your own ends!'

Georgina could have cried then. She could feel the tears stinging at the back of her nose and eyes. 'But Jennifer said——'

'She was afraid of you—and she had good reason to be! If you can black my eye, what could you do to her?'

'All right,' Georgina shouted at him. 'I didn't like the idea of your marrying Jennifer. I *hated* the idea! But I wouldn't have done anything to stop it—my quarrel has always been with you, not Jennifer. *Her* I love, and nothing would induce me to do anything to hurt her!'

'You're not going to get the opportunity,' he retorted.

It was strange, but miserable as she was, Georgina could still feel the warmth of the red-brick house's welcome as she reluctantly followed William inside. There was a pleasant smell of furniture polish and pieces of well kept copper twinkled at her from their place on the wall. Unlike the

Perry house, it was warm too, with a promise of comfortable chairs and hot crumpets for tea. She had once in her life been invited to tea with Mrs Ayres and that was what she had been given to eat, with piles of home-made jam and a great deal of shared laughter. William hadn't been there. He had just started to travel extensively in his job and Mrs Ayres had been proud of his achievements at such a young age. He had been working on a Commonwealth health project, she remembered, and he seemed to have been doing that ever since. It was a pity he was home at the moment.

'You can't make me do anything I don't want to,' she remarked as he pushed her ahead of him into the sitting-room. 'I'm not afraid of you!' There was a quiver in her voice that belied her words, but she held her head up high and gave him look for look. 'Just because you're as mad as hell——'

'Children, children,' Mrs Ayres rebuked them gently, coming in from the garden at the same moment. 'What are you bickering about now, you two?'

'Do we have to be bickering?' William asked her, his lips quirking with what could have been amusement.

'When have you ever done anything else?' his mother returned placidly. 'My dear boy, what have you done to your eye?'

'Ask Georgina!'

Mrs Ayres clicked her tongue, her eyes twinkling. 'Georgina, you *didn't*? It seems to have been remarkably effective.'

'He dared me to do it,' Georgina defended herself, trying not to allow her embarrassment to show. 'I'm terribly sorry, Mrs Ayres.'

'My dear girl, I'm in your corner! William has done nothing but provoke you ever since we first came to live here.'

Georgina cast a doubtful glance at William, but it was impossible to tell what he was thinking. His expression was sober and completely calm, not at all as though he was still in the grip of one of his cold rages.

'I've been provoking her to some effect this afternoon,' he told his mother, sounding almost amused. 'Didn't I tell you I hoped to marry the Perry girl?'

It was hard to tell who was the more astonished, Georgina or Mrs Ayres.

'Marry?' Georgina gasped, but the sound of her comment was completely lost in Mrs Ayres' whoop of joy.

'Darling William! I never thought you'd show so much sense! I'm ashamed to say that when you told me you were thinking about the Perry girl I jumped to the conclusion you meant Jennifer. I couldn't be more pleased!'

'Thank you, Mother.' His tone was so dry that Georgina blushed for him. 'I'm glad it meets with your approval.'

Georgina thought that Mrs Ayres, who must have known her son better than anyone else alive, should have been warned, but she was far too relieved to attempt to hide her joy from him—or Georgina.

'I know it's your life,' she rushed on, kissing her son warmly on the cheek, 'but Jennifer would never have been *my* choice for you. She would have bored you to death inside a fortnight of close proximity, whereas one never knows what to expect from Georgie, does one? So *much* more interesting! But I'm surprised you realised that for yourself, dear. I was so afraid you were blinded by Jennifer's fragile beauty—it won't last!—and would mistake one of her little girl's appeals for masculine sympathy as true love. The girl has never yet formed a stable relationship and, in my opinion, she never will.'

Georgina watched William's nostrils flare with fascinated dismay. Indeed, so intent was she on his reactions that she missed her own cue to deny the quite preposterous suggestion that she would ever marry William while she was still in her right mind and had breath in her body.

'We'll leave Jennifer out of this,' William said sternly to

his mother. 'It's easy to see you don't know her at all—only what you've heard about her from Georgina, who has never made the faintest effort even to be kind to her! That's something I mean to put a stop to in the future.'

The pleasure drained out of Mrs Ayres' face. 'William, you're not doing something foolish, are you?'

'Certainly not! It's all arranged, Mother. Jennifer is going to marry Duncan Radcliffe, and Georgie Porgie is going to marry me.'

'Have you asked her?' Mrs Ayres returned coldly.

'Georgina will do as she's told!'

'And put up with you calling her by that ridiculous name as well, I suppose? You should have grown out of teasing defenceless little girls by now, William. I'm disappointed in you.'

Georgina groaned inwardly. This was making bad worse with a vengeance. 'Mrs Ayres,' she began, 'I don't mind! I'm used to it! And—and William doesn't mean anything by it.' May God forgive me, she added to herself. 'Besides,' she went on, trying to sound lighthearted and able to take a joke against herself, 'the sting went out of that particular nursery rhyme a long time ago. Who wants to kiss the boys anyway? I'll settle for a grown man myself.'

'William?' his mother demanded caustically. 'You must be dotty, darling. If I were you I'd black his other eye for him and give him more of the same until he behaves himself.' A faint smile twisted her lips. 'I must say you did a good job. He's beginning to look like a prize-fighter—and not a very successful one at that! Does it hurt?' she asked, all concern, and then, when he nodded, briefly and without enthusiasm, 'Good!'

'I don't know about William,' Georgina said, intent on her own thoughts. 'He doesn't really mean to marry me, you know, and I certainly don't want to marry him!'

'Enlisting my mother's sympathy won't help you!' William shot at her. 'You'll marry me, Georgina——'

'You can't make me!'

'You think not?' Georgina's eyes fell before the dangerous glitter in his. 'I think I can. I can make things so hot for
you you'll be glad to marry me!'

Mrs Ayres looked so appalled by this claim that
Georgina felt sorry for her. She put a comforting hand on
the older woman's arm and said, 'You mustn't mind so
much, Mrs Ayres. William never means anything he says in
a rage—you know that.'

'I mean it this time, Georgie Porgie. This time you're
going to have a man to kiss and it won't be he who ends up
in tears. You're going to marry me and come with me to Sri
Lanka——'

'That'll be the day!' she scoffed.

'Indeed it will!' he retorted.

William would do nothing to put his mother's mind at rest.

'Don't hide behind her skirts,' he advised Georgina. 'It
won't do you any good.'

'But, William, I *like* your mother. Why do you have to
hurt her too?'

'She'll get over it. She'll forget *why* we got married once
the deed is safely done. By the time we present her with her
first grandchild she'll be convinced that the whole idea was
her own. She's always preferred you to Jennifer.'

Georgina tried not to allow the barb to hurt her. 'Is that
so odd?'

'To me it is. You have none of Jennifer's gentle and
appealing ways. Mother doesn't usually approve of violent
people.'

'How she must dislike you!' Georgina exclaimed.

He cast her an angry look. 'If I am violent with you it's
no more than you deserve,' he bit out. 'You'll find me quite
reasonable as long as you behave yourself. I think I know
how to handle you so that neither of us gets hurt too badly.
It's more than time that someone took you in hand!'

Georgina set her mouth in a stubborn line. 'I'm not going to marry you. I plan to marry someone else, as a matter of fact. I may have my faults, William dear, but your kind of arrogance is not part of my make-up. How will your pride enjoy having a wife who's in love with somebody else?'

'With whom?' He laughed without humour. 'Are you trying to tell me you have a boy-friend?'

'Why not?' she countered in commendably cool tones.

'Who is he?'

She opened her eyes wide, beginning to enjoy herself. 'Peter Anthony. I don't think you know him. Jennifer and I met him at a dance——'

'And you took him away from her, I suppose?'

Georgina sighed. 'I didn't have to. Impossible as you find it to believe, there are a few men in the world who don't give Jennifer a second glance. Not many, I grant you, but there are one or two.'

William frowned at her. 'And how far has this romance gone?' he demanded.

'That,' said Georgina, 'is none of your business.'

'It is now! Marry me you're going to, Georgina Perry, and although I don't relish the prospect of second-hand goods, it isn't going to put me off, if that's what you're hoping?'

Georgina's face flamed. 'Think what you like! I don't care!'

William raised his brows thoughtfully. 'I wonder why you do?' he murmured. 'You've always cared what I think. Why not admit it?'

Georgina shrugged. 'You flatter yourself—as always!' She flicked her fingers as close to his face as she could get. 'I don't care that much for what you think! And you won't find Peter as easy to bully as you do me. He's more of a man than you'll ever be!'

William threw back his head and laughed. 'Tell me that when you've been married to me for a week or more,' he said nastily. 'I've never had any complaints before.'

'I daresay nobody dared voice any,' Georgina retorted. 'Like Jennifer, they probably told their troubles to someone else. You're not a very sympathetic listener, William Ayres. In fact I don't find you sympathetic at all!'

'You don't have to, though, do you? Bullies in my experience always complain of being bullied when anyone dares put a stop to their activities. If you want me to be kind to you, the remedy is in your own hands. I'll be as kind to you as I think you deserve, no more, no less.'

Georgina rose to her feet. 'Thanks very much,' she said, the bitterness she was feeling rising like a geyser to the surface. 'I don't want you to be kind or not kind, or anything else! I just want you to leave me alone! I'm going home!'

He took her hands in his, pulling her into the circle of his arms. 'You're not going anywhere, my sweet——'

She stamped her foot at him, trying vainly to free her wrists from his clasp. 'Really, William, don't you think this joke has gone far enough? All right, you've given me a fine fright, which is presumably what you wanted to do, but I'm not frightened now. I've had it, and I've had you too!'

'Not yet you haven't, but you're going to.' He smiled at her with a gentleness that belied the pressure of his hands in the small of her back. 'You won't hanker after your Peter for long, Georgie Porgie, I promise you. If you'll let me, and by that I mean if you don't fight me every inch of the way, I'll make you very happy. It's a long time since I took a good look at you, but you're not as bad looking as I thought. Jennifer is so delicate-boned and fragile that she makes you look too solid and robust by comparison——'

Georgina achieved her ambition of stamping hard on his toe, followed by a fierce kick on the shins. She might just as well have saved herself the trouble, for William's only reaction was to laugh.

'Don't you want me to kiss you?' he teased her.

'I don't want to have anything to do with you!'

But she was very much aware of his hands on her back. They were warm and competent, holding her with an ease she had never come across before. Struggle as she would, she could not gain her freedom from him, and yet it was no effort to him to bring her closer still against him. Her heart beat increased its rhythm in a sudden excitement that she found quite inexplicable.

'You see,' he said in her ear, 'it isn't quite as you thought, is it? How do you like being on the receiving end for a change?'

It was a kiss such as she had never experienced before. His mouth commanded hers, parting her lips, and ignoring her spluttered protest. And then she didn't want to protest any more, nor did she want to escape from the pressure of his hands, or from the earthy, male smell of him at close quarters. It was as if she had no will of her own, but that her whole being had merged with his to give them both the greater satisfaction.

When he let her go, the reality of her position came rushing back to her and the tears came brimming into her eyes and down her cheeks. She wiped them away impatiently, hating herself for the feeling of acute loss that afflicted her.

'I told you it wouldn't be I who cried,' William's mocking voice reminded her.

'But you didn't say you wouldn't be able to resist saying I told you so!' she flared up at him. 'Nobody has ever kissed me against my will before, if you want to know. Are you surprised I'm upset?'

A crease appeared between his eyes, which were more green than gold at that moment. 'Peter can't be much of a man if he lets you make all the running. A woman has to be wooed, not left to take the initiative herself. Is he afraid of you too, Georgie Porgie?'

'Peter isn't afraid of anyone!'

He was silent for a long moment and Georgina eyed him covertly, wondering what he was thinking.

'In the same way that you're not afraid of me?' he questioned her at last. 'You can't make up your mind, can you? You're more attracted by my handling of you than you'll admit, Georgie. I don't believe anyone has assailed your heart and come close to bringing your defences tumbling down, my innocent. Tell me more about this Peter of yours.'

'There's nothing to tell.' Georgina gave him a mutinous look, recovering herself sufficiently to whip up her anger to boiling point again. 'I love him and I mean to marry him. That's all you need to know.' She hoped she didn't sound as guilty as she felt, for she could well imagine the unfortunate Peter's consternation if he could hear her. She thought it unlikely that he wanted their easy-going relationship to turn into anything more than the unemotional friendship it had been so far. He wouldn't like her using him as a defence against William, but, once she had explained things to him, she thought he would back her up until the danger was over. Peter was the most reliable person she knew and one of the best friends she had. It was true that sometimes she suspected he had got to know her in order to get closer to Jennifer, but she had never held this against him. He had seen through Jennifer with the greatest of ease and had pronounced her both shallow and wilful. Georgina hadn't wholly agreed with him, but she had been grateful that for once she had been found to be the greater attraction for one of the more personable young men of their mutual acquaintance.

'You must introduce him to me,' William suggested. 'I don't suppose you want to break it to him yourself that you aren't going to marry him after all?'

'But I am!' she protested.

'Oh no, my dear, you're not. It wouldn't *be* him for long, would it? You'd soon be casting an envious eye over

Duncan, and we'd all be back where we started, making the best of things after you've broken them into little pieces. No, Jennifer won't be safe from you until I have you firmly shackled to my side. I may not be able to give her anything else, but at least I mean to give her that!'

Georgina felt obliged to argue the point with him just one more time. 'What did I do to spoil things between you two?' she demanded. 'It wasn't I who forced Jennifer into Duncan's arms!'

'No, it was my arms you pushed her into, not Duncan's, but it all comes to the same thing. You've pushed Jennifer around for far too long. I'm going to give her her freedom. What she does with it is her own affair. I shall be occupied with controlling my own wife.' He smiled slowly, looking surprised. 'I even think I may enjoy it, young Georgie. Whatever else it is, it certainly won't be dull!'

'But, William, I don't want to marry you!' Georgina wailed.

'You will when you get used to the idea,' he returned calmly. 'My dear girl, susceptible to your own passions you've always been, but I don't believe anyone else has ever stormed your selfish little heart before today. Take care you don't lose it to me entirely if it amuses me to turn you into a loving wife after all.'

'William, I *hate you*!'

'Of course you do,' he answered in soothing tones. 'But hasn't anyone ever told you, Georgina dear, that hatred is the other side of the coin of love? Now, calm down and listen for a change. I have to be in Sri Lanka in three weeks' time. Can you be ready by then?'

Georgina seethed with frustrated fury. 'Am I supposed to answer that? How can I make it any clearer to you? I'm *not* going to marry you!'

'We can be married that same day in the morning,' he went on unperturbed. 'That'll give you the flight to get over the shock of finding that for once you haven't got your own way about something. Cheer up, Georgie, I won't hurry you into the responsibilities of married life once we're safely away from here. You'll have all the time you need before we come back to England and Jennifer. By that time you'll have forgotten that you were ever a reluctant bride and wife.'

'And what about Peter?'

William had the audacity to grin at her. 'I think I'll see Peter myself. If he's really set on marrying you, he'll probably take it better from me that you've changed your mind about him. I have an idea that you wouldn't throw your heart into the chore of telling him you're about to jilt him for Another.'

'You're right! Nor am I going to jilt him! I refuse to allow you to take my life over in any way. This is the twentieth century, William Ayres, and you'll soon find out you can't do it!'

For an instant he looked almost sorry for her. 'But I can, Georgie, that's the whole point. I can do it because you're the kind of girl who has been brought up to believe that she ought to marry her lover.' His eyes narrowed, giving him a wicked look that made her tremble inside. 'Would you prefer me to take you without marriage?' His eyes never left her face which he had forced up at an uncomfortable angle to make his point the more brutally. 'No, I thought not,' he said at last. 'At least you don't pretend that I couldn't do that too if I had a mind to! You're a poor loser, but you have a proud spirit. When I've finished with you, my sweet, you're going to be quite a woman!'

A lump formed in her throat and dissolved into a ball of hot wretchedness that robbed her of speech. All she could do was to thump her closed fists against his chest. She would have given anything to have poked him in the other eye at that moment, but her tears defeated her. Boxers wouldn't be boxers if they ever cried, she thought. Nor were they ever overwhelmed by a sense of desolation that occasionally afflicted all her sex. Life was so unfair!

'William, please let me go,' she whispered.

'I'm sorry, Georgie, but I can't do it. You won't find it so bad once you're used to the idea. And you'll enjoy living in Ceylon for a few months, if you'll allow yourself to. It's a beautiful island and a beautiful people to go with it. You'll love it!'

At any other time, under any other circumstances, that might have been true, but he must be mad if he thought she would enjoy anything in his company when she had thoroughly disliked him ever since she could remember. She opened her mouth to tell him so, but somehow the words didn't come out as she had intended. Instead a quite different question came tumbling out.

'What do you do when you go abroad for months together?'

He gave her a startled look. 'Don't you know? I'm an engineer. This time I'm going to Sri Lanka on a Commonwealth project to do with irrigation. It's one of the most interesting jobs I've ever tackled. I like having Commonwealth backing too. It's the sort of thing we ought to be doing to help the poorer members in the Third World, not making the gap ever wider between us. One day we'll pay for our greed and stupidity in the West if we don't do a great deal more of this sort of thing.' His golden eyes mocked her. 'One way or another, the selfish always pay in the end, or hadn't you noticed?'

Georgina's mouth trembled, betraying her hurt. 'Isn't there a parable about removing the beam from your own eye before you attempt the mote in your neighbour's? It could have been meant for you!'

He laughed out loud. It was a great gust of mirth that made her want to join in. 'My word, you never give in, do you?' The words ended in another bout of hilarity. 'Who ever would have thought the elder Perry girl had so much to her? Yet perhaps I should have guessed. You have a passionate mouth and enough fire in your belly for any man to handle. I wonder why I never noticed it before?'

Georgina made a face at him. 'My virtues will fade like candlelight before the sun when next you see Jennifer, no doubt. You can keep your compliments to yourself! I don't want to hear them!'

He kissed her lightly on the cheek. 'Jealous?' he asked in an intimate, deep murmur. 'You don't like it that I kissed Jennifer first, do you? Never mind, my sweet, at least you have the comfortable knowledge that from now on it will be you I'll be kissing.'

'Without love——'

'Love is only the icing on the cake,' he cut her off, his good humour gone. 'A good cake doesn't need to be covered in sentimental nonsense. It matures with time and never goes stale.'

'Cut and come again?' Georgina suggested wryly. 'That would never suit Jennifer, I'm afraid. She has a very sweet tooth.'

'It isn't Jennifer who has to be suited. All that matters on this occasion is what sort of a cake are you?'

Georgina thought she knew. A badly baked fruit cake that had sagged in the middle was how she felt. She could only hope that William would choke over one of the half-cooked crumbs!

# CHAPTER THREE

Georgina studied her husband sitting in the seat next door
to hers, but the dreadful unreality of the day refused to go
away. Not even the solid bulk of William's body could
make her believe she had given way and had actually said
the words that morning that had transformed her into being
his legal wife.

She would have held out if Peter hadn't betrayed her so
thoroughly and with such a lack of subtlety that she still
cringed when she thought about it. He had completely
ignored her frantic signals that she would explain matters
to him later. With a stupidity she had found deplorable, he
had willingly confessed to William that he had no romantic
interest whatsoever in Georgina Perry.

'We're just good friends,' he had said. Georgina had told
him afterwards that he might have found something more
original to say than that, but her erstwhile suitor had
merely looked hurt and puzzled and quite definitely lacking
in push.

'But, Georgie, you know we don't feel that way about
each other,' he had defended himself.

'*I* know,' she had agreed on a sigh. 'I would much sooner
that William hadn't known, though. If I don't look out, the
wretched fellow really will make me marry him!'

Peter had been embarrassed. 'How can he unless you let
him?' he asked unanswerably.

Georgina still didn't know how he had done it, but the
gold band on her finger refused to go away no matter how
often she tried to blink it out of sight. There was no doubt
about it, in the eyes of the law and in the sight of men she

had been transmogrified into Mrs William Ayres and it felt as though the whole bottom had fallen out of her world with a vengeance.

And vengeance had been what it was all about. She was too honest with herself to pretend that William's first judgment of her had changed to liking in the past few weeks. Far from it. If anything, he seemed to dislike her more now than ever. She wished she could say the same about him. She had disliked him, more had loathed everything about him, but in the whirlwind of the last few days, somehow she had found herself beginning to look for his arrogant presence. At first she had thought it was because he afforded her some protection from the avid curiosity of her whole family, but she had soon learned better. For some reason best known to her subconscious self, she just liked to have him around. Could it be that she was beginning to enjoy the verbal battles that was the only way they seemed able to converse with each other? If so, she had got everything she deserved: a marriage that was no marriage, and a husband who didn't even accord her the most grudging respect.

Her mother had been the other traitor who had made no bones about her joy in going over to the enemy's camp.

'My dear, I couldn't be more pleased!' she had crooned in ecstasy. 'I've always had a soft spot for William. Dear boy!'

'You don't think it might be a trifle awkward as he's only just stopped being engaged to Jennifer?' Georgina had said practically.

'I never took that particular relationship very seriously, dear,' her mother had replied, quite unperturbed. 'And nor should you. William knows what he's doing, I'm sure. Jennifer would never have done for him. Why, he looked and sounded like a grown man when he was only fifteen, and Jennifer—well, Jennifer is Jennifer, and we all love her dearly, but no one could describe her as *mature* yet in her love affairs. Why are you laughing, Georgie? Don't you think that's why William decided not to marry her after all?'

Georgina had regarded her mother with a little less than the usual affection she had for her. 'It wasn't William who broke things off, it was Jennifer. She prefers Duncan, or so she says. Hasn't she told you yet?'

Her mother's brow had creased thoughtfully. 'Duncan? You mean that little boy who was forever making her cry when you were all children? No, she hasn't said a single word to your father and me. She probably knows we wouldn't approve of her chopping and changing every few minutes—and certainly not to someone like Duncan! What a repulsive little boy he was!'

'I thought so,' Georgina admitted. 'Jennifer says she always rather liked him, only I used to bully them both into behaving badly. Is it true, Mother? Did I bully Jennifer?'

'Whoever gave you that idea? Your father used to say I made you look after Jennifer too much, and it would serve me right if you went through one of those tiresome bossy phases elder sisters do sometimes, but I can't say I ever noticed that you did. The only person you ever fought with was William. You turned into a regular shrew every time he came around.' She had laughed softly. 'The magic chemistry already beginning to work between you seems the most likely solution to that! It seems ridiculous now, but when your father and I were courting we used to fight like wildcats too, but since we got married we've seldom had a cross word. *That's* how it will be with you and William, you see!'

Georgina, unable to follow her on this particular romantic flight of fancy, had merely looked sulky. 'A quiet wedding would be much more suitable. I'm sure William would prefer a register office——'

'Certainly not! This is your big day, darling! William and I have already agreed you'll be married in the village church with all your friends about you. He doesn't approve of hole-and-corner weddings any more than I do. They lack conviction.'

'I lack conviction,' Georgina had said sadly.

'Very proper in a bride,' her mother had put in quickly. 'You can rely on William to more than make up for any reservations you have, however. I do like a man who knows his own mind!'

Georgina had made one last attempt to win her mother over to her side. 'What about Jennifer?' she had asked bluntly. 'She won't like it——'

Mrs Perry hadn't even bothered to look up from her sewing. 'Jennifer will have to live with her own decisions,' she had said. And then she had looked up, holding her daughter's whole attention by the simple expedient of waving her needle in her face. 'If you let Jennifer ruin this for you, Georgina, I'll never forgive you!' she had declared with unusual vigour. 'William is everything I hoped for you, and if you throw his love away in a foolish gesture of concern for Jennifer, he's unlikely to give you a second chance to make a fool of him. Be happy with him, darling, and forget all about everything else. If you don't, you'll be storing up a great deal of unhappiness for yourself. Love denied turns to bitterness more often than it can be sublimated into service for others.'

'I haven't said I'm in love with William,' Georgina had protested.

'I can't imagine your marrying him for any other reason!' her mother had retorted. 'Don't be a silly girl! Of course you're in love with him! So marry him and be happy, and give over worrying about Jennifer, do! The Jennifers of this world are very well able to look after themselves.'

Georgina hoped she was right. She had been too busy bending to the wind that was William these last few days to have given much thought to her sister, but she had spoken to her the night before. Jennifer had been out with Duncan and had come in late. There had been a hectic flush in her cheeks and her eyes had sparkled with the excitement of the evening's dancing.

'Will you give this letter to William tomorrow?' she had asked Georgina.

'You'll probably see him before I do,' Georgina had answered. 'Mother has an idea it's unlucky for a bride to see her groom before they meet in church.'

'But the letter is for afterwards, darling,' Jennifer had drawled, a malicious smile on her lips. 'We don't want him to carry you off to the wilder shores of the Indian Ocean still wondering about his first love, do we? It's only to say I don't bear either of you any resentment for leaving me behind without giving a thought as to whether I shall be happy without you both.'

'But if you're going to marry Duncan——?'

Jennifer had shrugged her shoulders. 'Am I? William was a lot less boring than Duncan, if you want to know, only he was always going away. You're welcome to him!'

*The letter.* Georgina hadn't given it a thought from that moment till this. She opened her handbag and scrabbled round inside, looking for it.

'Are you going to be sick?' William asked her.

'No. Why?' She found the pale mauve envelope with a sigh of relief. For a moment she had thought she had forgotten to transfer it from one bag to the other, and she could well imagine Jennifer's anger if she had forgotten to give her precious letter to William.

'You look a trifle green,' he observed.

'I thought I'd lost Jennifer's letter.' She handed it to him. 'It's for you.'

'So I see,' he said dryly. He examined the envelope with care, noting the way the flap had been tucked into the back and the way Jennifer had written BY HAND in the top left-hand corner, in huge, flamboyant capitals, and William down below, underlining it with a strong double line. 'Have you read it?'

'Of course not. It's addressed to you.'

'You might have been curious as to what she had to say to me now that I'm your husband.' He pulled the single sheet out of the envelope and opened it slowly. 'Weren't you a little bit curious?' he asked Georgina, a funny little smile playing round his lips.

'If I was, I managed to restrain it by forgetting all about it. I thought I'd left it in my other handbag——' She broke off as his expression changed to one of cold contempt.

'I don't believe you,' he said.

'Why not? What does she say?' Georgina demanded. She snatched the letter out of his hand and began to read it for herself. It was dated the day before yesterday and began, Darling William—— 'I don't understand!' Georgina said brokenly. 'I don't understand it!'

'Don't you? It seems quite simple to me. Jennifer changed her mind again and tried to let me know she'd made a terrible mistake and very much hoped I would take her back after all. Why did you do it, Georgina? Why? It wasn't as though you wanted to marry me yourself. Or did you? Is that why you deprived us of our chance of happiness?'

'But it wasn't like that! She told me to give you the letter *after* the wedding. I made a point of telling her that Mother wouldn't allow me to see you before the service began. Jennie said it was to tell you that she didn't bear you any resentment for marrying me.'

'That isn't what she says there,' William pointed out.

'I can't help what she wrote to you! I'm telling you what *happened*!'

'And I don't believe you.'

Georgina went very white. For one awful moment she thought she was going to faint. 'I don't care what you believe! I don't tell lies!'

'Meaning Jennifer does? Forgive me, my dear wife, if I choose to believe the woman I love. Her record gives her a credence which yours does not!'

'You don't have to stay married to me!' Georgina cried out. 'An annulment would suit me just fine!'

'Oh, Georgie, stop whistling in the dark! Why suppress the letter and marry me in the first place if it's an annulment you want?'

Georgina gave way to an hysterical laugh. 'Why indeed? That ought to prove it to you that I didn't read the letter in advance. If this isn't just like Jennifer! How she loves to stir things up!'

'And you don't?'

She sobered. 'No, I don't think I do. I haven't the imagination to make the most of my chances. If I had, I would have read your letter then and there and found out what Jennifer was up to. One is at such a disadvantage when one expects everyone to behave by one's own standards. You'd have thought I'd have learned better by now.' It was a cry from the heart, but William showed no sign of taking it as such.

'Very clever,' he remarked. 'If I didn't know you better I might have believed you. God, Georgina, I didn't think even you hated me as much as that!'

'You've never done anything to make me like you very much, so why shouldn't I? Not that I did! Not because of you, but because of me. I wouldn't *stoop*——'

'Words, Georgie. I think you'd do almost anything to get even with me—perhaps you think you're justified, who knows? But I can promise you you won't enjoy the fruits of your triumph! Marriage can be heaven or hell, my dear. I was going to try and make it as pleasant as possible for you; I now feel relieved of any such obligation. My vengeance can be as bitter as yours—and a great deal more intimate!'

She closed her eyes, trying not to listen. 'Why don't you

let me go and marry your marvellous Jennifer, if that's what you want to do?' she asked him.

He was quiet for so long that she thought he hadn't heard her and she opened her eyes to see what he was doing. His face was very close to hers in what could easily have been mistaken as a loving gesture. Only she could see the cold hardness of his eyes.

'What I have, I hold, Georgina Ayres,' he said slowly. 'Isn't that what I promised you this morning? *To have and to hold, from this day forward? For ever? For the rest of your life, my dear, dear wife!*'

She closed her eyes again, giving herself up to misery. What a fool she had been to marry him, she thought. What a *fool*! Perhaps she had said it aloud, though she had said it to herself.

'Why did you marry me, Georgie?' he asked her. 'I couldn't really have forced you to it, as you very well know. What made you actually say the fatal words?'

The pain of her unhappiness collected as a lump in her chest and the back of her throat felt as stiff as a board.

'I think I wanted to,' she answered. 'I wanted to see Sri Lanka.'

'And to be my wife?'

'I don't know,' she confessed. 'I tried not to think about it. I thought you'd find out—I thought you might be kinder once we were away from home. I don't know what I thought!'

To her surprise he smiled at that. 'Very likely! Poor Georgie, do you always hit out before you think, even when it's yourself who gets hurt?'

Her gaze flew to the yellow smudge that was all that was left of the black eye she had given him.

'Only with you,' she confided. 'You're the only person I've ever hated.' She swallowed, summoning up all the reserves she had at her disposal. 'I wish I were as nasty as you think me,' she said passionately, 'and I'd make you wish you'd never been born!'

His smile widened. 'You can try,' he invited her.

He turned away from her, settling back in his seat, and began to read the printed menu he had found in the pocket in front of him. 'Good lord, they don't mean us to starve! Two dinners and three breakfasts! That ought to hold us for a few hours after we get there!'

Georgina slept fairly well until the vast aeroplane prepared to come down at Bombay. She had watched the pirate film that had been provided for their entertainment, but had been unable to keep her mind on the rather trite story. She had enjoyed the fencing, though. She had done some fencing herself while she had been away at college and she found that that knowledge added to rather than detracted from the carefully staged fights on the screen.

She had taken some pleasure in telling William that the heroine was very much better with the foil than the hero.

'Are you a female chauvinist as well?' he had asked her.

'I am when she has to work quite so hard not to disarm him entirely,' she had retorted. 'She could take him apart any time she chose!'

'It wouldn't do much for the story line,' he had observed. 'The helpless maiden rescuing the knight in shining armour doesn't sound right. That's the trouble with women these days, they won't stick to their own role in life.'

'Wailing and weeping on the sidelines went out with crinolines,' she had said with satisfaction. 'We've learned it's better to rely on ourselves since then. It's better to make one's own mistakes.'

'And have two heads in every household?'

She had considered the point carefully, sure he had laid a trap for her. 'I suppose it works better when the man is the head and the woman the heart of the family, but some men abdicate their responsibilities and then the woman has to step in or the children suffer.'

He had picked up her hand in his, examining the ring on her finger. 'I shan't abdicate my responsibilities,' he had said.

It wasn't possible to get any accurate impressions of what Bombay was really like. Circling over it as they came down to refuel at the International Airport, it looked much smaller than Georgina had imagined it to be. But then, from the air, all India looked the same dun colour and practically uninhabited. The teeming millions of India were nowhere to be seen.

'Next stop Colombo,' said William.

'And then where?'

'Nowhere today. I'll be picking up a car tomorrow and then we'll drive up to Kandy and settle in. Today, we'll sleep off the flight and catch up with ourselves.'

'And see Colombo?' she prompted him.

He shook his head. 'There'll be plenty of time for that. Don't look like that, Georgie. We're going to do things my way and it simply doesn't pay to rush about the moment you get off an aeroplane after a long flight. You'll see the whole island before we go home, I promise you. Only not today.'

She looked up at him through her lashes. 'You're still angry,' she accused him. 'It will take more than that to spoil my pleasure, though. Everyone says Sri Lanka is a beautiful place, and even you can't make it ugly just to spite me!'

He was taken aback by the attack. 'My dear Georgina, hasn't anyone ever told you about the effects of jet lag? If you want to make yourself ill, by all means take yourself off and visit the museum, or anywhere else you want to go. I'm going to bed!'

She wondered if she wanted to brave an unknown city in

an unknown world by herself and came to the conclusion she didn't.

'You're sure it isn't because you want to ruin things for me?' she demanded, still suspicious.

'My revenge will be a great deal more subtle than that,' he told her. 'Enjoy Sri Lanka all you can, it's your marriage to me which is going to be your prison. For once, you're going to pay for taking something away from Jennifer out of the rather despicable envy you've always had for her. To be an unloved wife is more of a punishment than to deny you any amount of sightseeing, as you'll find out!'

He made a formidable enemy, she thought. 'You mean we're each going to live our own lives——?'

'What on earth makes you think that?' he exploded.

'You said unloved. I thought you meant—unloved.'

'I see.' His grim amusement cut her to the quick. 'Making love is a euphemism that should never be used in our kind of marriage, but I don't see why I should deny myself the pleasures of your body for such a quixotic reason, do you?'

'I think you're horrid!'

'So you've said before. It becomes tedious. It would be more wifely if you kept your opinion of me to yourself in future.'

'While you can say what you like about me? You'd better look out that I don't black your other eye for you! A fine fool you'd look if I did!'

'By all means try if you think you can, but to be fore-warned is to be forearmed. I might get in first. Have you thought of that?'

'You mean you'd hit *me*?' She could scarcely believe her ears. Surely William wasn't the kind of man who would hit a woman?

'There are times when I'd give anything to wallop you black and blue, but I don't suppose I will unless badly provoked, and you won't do that, will you, Georgie Porgie?

I'll make a pact with you: if you keep your fists to yourself, so will I. Agreed?'

She sniffed. 'You talk as if I were always punching you in the face,' she complained.

'Once was enough,' he said dryly. 'I won't be as forbearing another time, my ruffian wife.'

'No? I suppose you'll think of Jennifer and let fly? What a pity she won't be there to see it!'

He snorted in derision. 'Could be! And you won't have my mother in your corner to cheer you on either, which should reduce your chances somewhat. You'd better make up your mind to behave yourself like the lady you were brought up to be!'

She managed a wide, insouciant smile, to show him how little she cared about his threats. 'I'll see,' she compromised. 'It was such a splendid black eye last time that the joy of it may last me for a long time to come, but I'm not making any promises, you understand? Even ladies slap down their menfolk when the occasion demands it, you know.'

'The operative word is slap, my dear, not punch in the eye!'

The wry humour of his words appealed to her, but not for worlds would she have let him see it. 'Why don't you go outside and stretch your legs?' she suggested to him.

His only answer was to sit down again in the seat beside her, hunching his shoulders in an attempt to get a little more comfortable. She sank back herself, pushing her legs out in front of her. Why it should matter to her that he should choose to stay, she could not tell, but his presence lit a small candle of happiness inside her. If he would only forget Jennifer for a few days he might see her as a person in her own right. If only— It was the most useless phrase she knew. He didn't want to forget Jennifer and, now that he couldn't have her, he was intent on exacting his revenge for his disappointment from her. If only he would believe her about the letter! If only—

'I'm going to write to Jennifer,' she said aloud. 'I'll tell her you got her letter safely. You can read it before I send it, if you like.'

'I don't believe in flogging dead horses. Put Jennifer out of your mind, Georgie, and I'll try to do the same. We're stuck with each other, so we may as well make the best of things.'

She pursed up her lips. 'And know you're wishing I were Jennifer whenever you come near me? Why should I put up with that?'

'I'm more likely to treat you gently if I do imagine you to be Jennifer! But you needn't worry. No one would mistake you for her in their right senses. And you won't mind half as much as you think you will. If you were honest, you would admit you liked my kisses very well indeed. Nor have you any excuse for mistaking my intentions towards you, like you did Peter's. A trifle slow in the uptake, your gentleman friend, wouldn't you say?'

Georgina would have said a great deal more than that, but she restrained herself nobly. 'He's not such a fool as all that!'

'My dear girl, you should have seen his face when I suggested to him you were hoping to marry him. He wasn't worthy of your undoubted talents!'

She blushed with pleasure. 'What talents?' she asked hopefully.

'That would be telling!' His mouth twitched. 'You haven't had as much experience of the opposite sex as you pretend, Georgie Porgie. The time for kissing mere boys has gone now you have a man of your own. You'll need all the talents you possess to cope with him!'

'With you?' She felt suddenly humble in the face of the challenge he held out to her. He must feel *something* for her after all.

'Since Peter failed you, I'm the only man you've got,' he

drawled, getting slowly to his feet. 'I won't have you playing around with anyone else.'

He disappeared down the aisle towards the open door of the plane, exchanging a laughing word with one of the fresh hostesses who had come on board a few minutes before. Georgina saw the quick interest on the hostess's face and wondered if every female felt the same way when they saw his shaggy good looks and the distinctly masculine look in his gold-brown eyes. Was it no more than the automatic, feminine reaction to any personable man that she felt for him? Was that what had been the matter with her ever since she had discovered she didn't dislike him half as much as she had thought she did? But no, that was ridiculous. He wasn't the kind of man who had ever attracted her in the past. Her type had always been the well-read, gentle, academic sort, not an engineer who liked to get his hands dirty and who didn't give a damn how he won just as long as he did. That was the William she knew! A man too arrogant to be borne!

Yet when he came back to her there was no doubt but that her heart beat faster.

'We're about to have breakfast again,' he said, throwing himself back into his seat.

'*Again?*'

'It's the last time before Colombo,' he said solemnly. 'You'd better make the most of it.'

She giggled in a way she seldom did, but which Jennifer did all too often, and was rewarded by a sharp look from her husband.

'You don't do that often enough,' he told her.

'There hasn't been much to laugh about recently,' she reminded him.

'We'll have to change that.' His eyes lit with a purely masculine glint that shook her to the core, it was so unexpected. 'What kind of things do you find funny, Georgie?'

'Not you!' She turned her head away and made a play of

fanning herself with the paperback she held in her hand. 'It's hot in here, isn't it?'

He put out a hand and took the book away from her, glancing at its title as he did so. Apparently he approved of the title, for he turned it over and began to read the blurb on the back.

'Coward,' he murmured. 'What do you think I can do to you in a public plane?'

'I hadn't considered the matter,' she replied with a lift to her chin.

He chuckled. 'Liar! Are you reading this?'

'Yes, I am!' She took it back from him and, finding her place, buried her nose in it to such good effect that she barely noticed the shutting of the doors and consequently missed the last sight she might have had of Bombay as they took off and circled southwards over the city.

It didn't seem long after that she had her first glimpse of Sri Lanka. The white sands that fringed the coconut plantations shone brightly in the sun, promising a welcome of the kind that usually only travel brochures can offer, and then only by dint of some very careful photography.

Georgina put her hand on William's arm, shutting out the scene down below her. 'Is it all like that?' she breathed.

'Round the coast it is.' He looked at her more closely. 'What's the matter?'

'I'm frightened,' she said. 'I wish I hadn't come! And, more than anything, I wish I wasn't here with you!'

'It looks pretty good to me,' he said.

It looked better than that to her. That was the trouble, though she could hardly tell him that. She was afraid of losing her heart to both the island and to him. *If she hadn't done so already.*

'I want to go home,' she said.

# CHAPTER FOUR

The hotel was, frankly, a disappointment to Georgina. She had expected something more in keeping with the way of life she had glimpsed from the minibus that had taken them from the airport into Colombo, but once within the air-conditioned portals of the hotel they could have been anywhere in the world.

'You'll feel better when you've had some sleep,' William told her with such confidence that a little of her own fright ebbed away. 'Sit down over there while I check in and cash some money and then we'll go upstairs to bed.'

But even that promise seemed to hold overtones of other, less desirable, possibilities, and she was a little afraid she would lose sight of him altogether in the comings and goings of parties of French and German tourists who seemed to be constantly on the move in the gigantic foyer of the hotel. She wished she had asked William if she could have had a cup of tea while she waited, for despite the many meals of the night, she was thirsty, but she didn't like to join him in the queue where he was standing.

When he had finally finished his business and came over to her waving the key, she was obsessed by the idea of having something to drink.

'William, do let's have tea out on the terrace,' she suggested.

'We will this evening,' he promised her. 'Right now I want to get upstairs before the luggage arrives. You'll have to make do with water.'

'From the tap?'

He shook his head. 'Maybe, here, but don't even drink from the tap outside of Colombo. You can tell, more or less,

50

if the water is potable or not by whether the hotel provides a flask in the bedrooms. Coming?'

She went with him to the lift, a trifle bemused by the many exhibitions that were being housed in the various public rooms of the hotel.

'Still wanting to go home?' William inquired as they stepped into the lift.

She watched him press the button, knowing that he thought she was being silly. 'I suppose you feel at home in places like this?' she hazarded. 'I don't think I've ever stayed in a large hotel before. I read somewhere that such places have a well-oiled cosmopolitan atmosphere, but I've never been part of the international jet set before, so it just seems frighteningly impersonal. Positively gruesome!'

He laughed. 'Still hankering after going sightseeing?'

'No,' she admitted, 'I'll settle for some sleep. I expect the beds will be comfortable anyway——' She broke off, playing nervously with the strap of her handbag. 'Have we got two rooms?' she asked abruptly.

'Married couples usually share a room,' he responded calmly. 'But cheer up, Georgina, you'll have your bed to yourself for today and tonight.'

She expelled her breath in a sigh of naked relief. Indeed, she felt sufficiently reassured to answer him in his own manner. 'I hope you don't snore,' she said. 'Jennifer does. When we've been away together, I never would share a room with her because of it. But perhaps no one has told you whether you do or not?'

'I've never had any complaints,' he said dryly.

The lift doors opened and he stepped out before her, marching off down the red-carpeted corridor with an air of knowing exactly where he was going. Georgina followed more slowly. It came to her that she really knew very little about her husband, or the kind of life he led when he was away from home. There could have been any number of women who had shared more with him than she ever would.

The thought of them disturbed her, distressing her out of all proportion to their probable importance to him and therefore to her.

He unlocked and threw open the door to their room, waiting for her to come up to him. When he touched her arm she felt a wave of excitement shoot through her and she hastened her step to get away from him. She was being ridiculous! More men than she could count had made a similar gesture towards her and she had never felt the slightest thing more than a brief gratitude for their courtesy. Her innards had never, *never* turned to liquid fire, not even when some of them had kissed her.

It was a typical, impersonal hotel room, and yet she thought she would never forget the way it had looked to her then. William swept back the curtains to reveal a view of the sea and the Parliament buildings outside the double-glazed windows. There was a small notice stuck on to the glass asking guests not to open the window when the air-conditioning was switched on, and she examined it with a care that she hoped would hide her nervousness from him.

'William——'

He looked up, his eyes quizzical. 'Georgina.'

'I'm sorry I'm not Jennifer. I mean, I know you're not getting any more pleasure out of this than I am. Wouldn't it be better——'

'No.'

'*Why not?*'

'I'm not pretending Jennifer wouldn't have been a better choice, but you'll do, Georgie Porgie. I'll see that you do!'

'One can't make oneself love to order,' she said, rubbing at the paper notice on the window with her finger.

'Who said anything about love?'

She sighed. 'It's hopeless trying to talk to you,' she complained. 'If you aren't in love with Jennifer why did you want to marry her?'

'I don't consider that any of your business,' he returned

coolly. 'If you want to use the bathroom first, my dear, you'd better hurry up before my chivalrous instincts are overcome by need.'

'Have you got any?'

'Chivalrous instincts? I have a few. If you give up your bossy ways, you may be surprised.' He grinned maliciously at her. 'Are you going to try me out?'

Tears—tears, she hoped of fatigue—flooded into her eyes and she blinked them angrily away, disappearing into the bathroom. For a long time she stood in the small space that was all that was provided and fought to regain control over herself. She would feel better after a good sleep, she told herself, and therefore the sooner she got into bed the better, but until the luggage came up she had no nightdress with her. She undressed to her petticoat, paused, and then went the whole hog, taking a quick shower while she was about it. She put her petticoat back on, draping her towel about her shoulders for added protection.

William's eyebrows rose when he saw her. 'Is that for my benefit?' he asked. 'The female form holds no surprises for me, Georgie Porgie.'

'It's for *my* benefit!' she retorted.

His eyes travelled over with appreciation. 'Your modesty becomes you, but it doesn't cover you very well.' He watched the burning blush travel up the back of her neck as she turned away from him, seeking the safety of the bed nearest the window. 'Relax, Georgie. In that department, at least, you're every bit as good as your sister!'

She flung herself into bed. 'I'm better, if you want to know!' she declared violently. 'Even Jennifer admits that!'

'Does she, though? Then why try to hide yourself away? I wouldn't have said timidity, or coyness either, was a vice of yours.'

She gritted her teeth, hiding her face in the pillow. 'I'm not accustomed to sharing a room,' she said in muffled tones. 'Leave me alone!'

He stood over her, laughing. 'Very affecting. You'll get used to it, Georgie Porgie.' He bent down and kissed the exposed skin below her ear, ruffling her hair as he did so. 'Sleep well, little one!'

'I'm not a child!' she flared, frightened by the burning excitement his touch induced in her.

'No, you're not, so if you want to sleep don't press your luck, my girl!' He placed the back of his hand against her cheek in a surprisingly tender gesture. 'We'll talk this evening if that's what you want. I don't suppose you've ever seen the famous green flash that follows the sun's going down in the tropics? That'll be one thing you can look forward to without any fear of the consequences.'

She wanted to put up her hand to his, but she had no right to do so. Instead she turned on her back and looked steadily up at him.

'I'm not afraid of you, William Ayres. I'll never be afraid of you! So don't flatter yourself that I am!'

He smiled. 'If you were, you'd die sooner than admit it, wouldn't you, Georgie Porgie? What a strange girl you are! I'm glad I brought you with me if I couldn't have Jennifer. Life with you is unlikely to be dull, whatever else it may be!'

Her eyes followed him as he walked away from her and went into the bathroom in his turn. Would she be second best for ever and ever? she wondered. As far as he was concerned it seemed likely. What a fool Jennifer had been to want someone else when she could have had him and his love as well! How could anyone prefer a man like Duncan when they could have had all that? Georgina fingered her cheek where she could still feel the sensation of his touch and marvelled at the painful surge of emotion that engulfed her. She didn't even like him! She must concentrate on that and on all the things about him that had never failed to irritate her in the past. But she could still feel the gentleness of his skin against hers when she fell into an uneasy slumber, and it was of him that she dreamed until his hand on her shoulder shook her awake many hours later.

'Is it time to get up already?' she asked, confused.

'If you want that cup of tea it is.' He shook her again. 'No going back to sleep again now! You didn't even wake up when the suitcases arrived. Do you always sleep like one dead?'

She blinked, her dreams merging into real life for a delicious, uncertain moment. But then she saw that he was already dressed and that his expression was one of impatience rather than tenderness.

'You should have woken me sooner,' she said. 'Why don't you go down and order the tea and I'll follow as soon as I'm dressed?'

But still he lingered. 'How long will you be?'

She glanced at her watch. 'Ten minutes?'

He smiled at that. 'That'll be the day! If you're much over half an hour there won't be any tea for you; an hour and I'll come up and get you!'

'I'll be ready in ten minutes!' she claimed. She screwed up her eyes, watching him through her lashes to see what his reaction would be to that. It was impossible to tell. She hoped that her own racing pulses were as invisible to him. She had been so sure that he had been about to lean over and kiss her, which was ridiculous in itself, but what was worse was that she had wanted him to do exactly that and she had wanted it in every fibre of her being. 'You'd have made a good slave master,' she added, 'only slaves are self-made, you know. I read an article about it. If you think free, you are free!'

'Stone walls do not a prison make—and all that? I shouldn't rely on the theory too heavily if I were you,' he advised.

'But you're not me! Will you kindly stop standing over me in that impossible way and go away! I'll never get dressed with you looking on. I'm entitled to my privacy and I mean to have it!'

His eyebrows rose, a gleam of amusement entering the gold of his eyes. 'My dear girl, if you carry on like this often I shall begin to think I've disappointed you in some way. What were you dreaming of when I woke you, or would that be telling?'

She cast her gaze down to his neatly polished shoes. 'You'd find it a dead bore if I did tell you,' she said. 'There's nothing more boring than other people's dreams. Besides, I can never remember mine.'

'Pity. They might tell you something interesting about yourself——'

'Am I so difficult to understand?'

'You'd best ask yourself that. Do you understand yourself?' His lips twitched. 'Do you begin to know what it is you want out of life?'

'Oh yes,' she answered gravely. 'I've always known that. William——'

'Uh-huh.'

'Go away.'

But when he had gone she didn't get straight out of bed. She lay there, with her hands under her head, wondering what it was he had said that she had found so shattering. Or was it what she had said? Or dreamed about him? That was the most likely explanation! Her whole being had been expecting his caress and it had been like falling into ice-cold water to have it denied her when she had been jolted out of her sleep into reality. Had he known? Was that what he had meant when he had asked her if she knew what she wanted from life? The thought was humiliating in the extreme, in fact it was quite unbearable and most unlikely. If she were sensible she would put it out of her mind and go and join him on the terrace for tea. There was nothing in their last exchange for her to get hot and bothered about; it was merely her imagination playing tricks—

But William had known many, many women. He probably knew better than she did the unconscious signs a woman made when she was attracted to someone, even if she didn't want to be attracted to him. Well, she would just have to disabuse him of any thought that *she*— Supposing he had kissed her? It would have been no big thing in her life! *She didn't like William!*

She chose a pretty flowered dress from her suitcase and donned it in a rush, determined not to give him cause to gloat over being longer than she had specified before she joined him on the terrace. It was a very feminine dress with frothy lace at the neck and cuffs. Surely no one could think her hard and bossy in such a dress? To her own eyes she looked as vulnerable as she felt: afraid of William and afraid that she was going to get hurt, but when she smiled she looked a shade more confident. She would have to smile a great deal that evening, she recommended to herself. She would be cool, casual, and charming, and he would never suspect the turmoil that was going on inside her.

She squirted some scent on to the back of her neck and down the front of her dress and then sniffed the air anxiously, afraid she had been too lavish. Some people had an aversion to the cheaper scents that flooded the world's markets and she had never been able to afford anything else. What did William think about things like that? She tossed her head at her reflection in the glass, telling herself it was sheer snobbery to care, and hurried on her way downstairs before she could think of anything else to worry about. She could do without such niggling doubts if she wanted to carry the day with William. With him, she needed every scrap of confidence she could command. And yet—and yet it felt that her whole being burgeoned into a new life when she saw him, his long legs stretched out in front of him, sitting at one of the far tables on the terrace.

'Eleven and a half minutes,' he growled at her as she sat down beside him.

'One and a half minutes to find you sitting right over here,' she retorted, flashing a determined smile in his direction, and then wishing that she hadn't, since he was bound to know that it was as false as was the lightness of her tone.

'You still look a bit washed out,' he commented, looking her over.

'How charming of you to notice,' she returned. 'I could say the same for you, but I won't. I'll compliment you on your choice of shirt instead.'

'Meaning that you hoped I'd notice you had on a Jennifer-style dress? Well, I had noticed. Did you steal it out of her wardrobe when she wasn't looking?'

Georgina looked far out to sea, her whole attention on the setting globe of the sun, now gold, now enormous and scarlet as it slid down into the purple-grey of the water.

'Jennifer's clothes don't fit me,' she said mildly. 'Hadn't you noticed that I'm larger round the bust?'

'It can't make that much difference!' He studied her with renewed interest. 'Perhaps it does at that! You haven't Jennie's delicate air, but you make an exciting handful for all that!' He noted her blush with satisfaction, his smile adding a cruel twist to his lips. 'Is that what you really wanted me to notice?'

'No, I'm quite indifferent to your excitements.' She leaned forward, staring so hard at the setting sun her eyes hurt. 'When does the green flash come?'

'Just as the sun disappears. Any second now. Wait for it—*now*! Did you see it?'

'Yes—yes, I did.' She sounded almost as surprised as she felt that she had actually seen the flash on the horizon that had saluted the departure of the setting sun. 'I didn't really believe it would happen. Why does it?'

He started to explain it to her, but soon realised she

wasn't listening to him. 'You don't really want to know, do you?' he muttered, disgruntled.

'It might destroy the magic,' she explained.

He gave her a wry look. 'Who would have thought our Georgie Porgie was a romantic at heart? You've given few signs of it before! What did you learn at that college of yours, by the way? Jennifer seemed to think it was something about making bricks without straw? Not very likely, I thought.'

Georgina deliberately relaxed her clenched fists. 'Women seldom take up building,' she said.

He laughed. It wasn't a pleasant sound. 'I can well imagine you as a "bricky", though, carrying hods of bricks through the mud and wet concrete of a building site, proving yourself as good or better than any man!'

Georgina forced a smile. 'A regular Amazon, in fact? I rather like that! When one's small, one likes to be thought bigger than one is, and to be a pint-sized Amazon is better than to be a quart-sized, besotted humbug——'

'Like me?'

She shrugged. 'If the cap fits,' she suggested sweetly, 'you know what to do with it.'

He looked suddenly thoughtful. 'I hadn't realised how small you are,' he said at last. 'How tall are you? Five-one? Five-two? Jennifer must be a good three inches taller——'

'She weighs more too!' Georgina pointed out, not without malice.

'Not when I first knew you,' William remembered. 'You were a very solid little girl.'

'That,' Georgina said briskly, 'was a long, long time ago. You should catch up with the times, my lad. You live far too much in the past. Anyone would think you were middle-aged, you're so nostalgic about the days of your youth! Still, I suppose everyone feels the same about their first love—only most of us grow up and go on to bigger and better things.'

William eyed her soberly. 'What did you learn at college?'

'Not psychology. Design and commercial art.' She lifted her chin, congratulating herself on getting the best of the latest skirmish between them. 'Hence the bricks without straw, I suppose. Jennifer doesn't approve of artists selling their talents on the open market. In her opinion they ought to be starving in a garret, or living in the shadow of some patron. I'm not that romantic!'

'Nor am I,' he agreed unexpectedly. 'That's why I became an engineer. I like to see good, solid, practical results to my work. You don't get that with pure science. It's the technicians, the engineers, who've made civilisations work, right from the very beginning—far more than the so-called scientific bods. Nor do I live in the past much. My work is fashioning the future, and that's where most of my thoughts are.'

'And in your private life?'

'That's a more difficult question to answer,' he admitted. 'One gets caught up in things. That's why I wanted to bring Jennifer out here.' He hesitated, chewing on the inside of his lip. 'She has a gentle, loving nature and that's what Celine needs most at this moment.' His lips tightened. 'Celine is the past all right. She lives there all the time, no matter what anyone does to try and give her a future.' He sighed. 'Jennifer would have been good for Celine.'

'Celine?' Georgina felt completely lost. 'Who is Celine?'

William stared morosely out to sea. 'I inherited her from her father. He was a good friend of mine until he was killed by a flash flood in Australia. I'd promised him if anything happened to him I would take care of Celine for him. She's a pretty girl, but not quite all there, if you know what I mean. She was completely normal when her mother was alive, but her death affected her very badly. After that she never seemed to grow up. She's nearly twenty now, but she sounds and behaves as if she were half that age. I thought Jennifer would be good for her.'

Georgina spread her fingers on her knees. 'Did Jennie know about Celine?'

'No. I thought it would be enough for her to find out about her after we were married. Whatever happens, you see, I can't ditch Celine now.'

Georgina surveyed him in silence for a moment. 'It's a good thing you married me and not Jennie, then,' she said. 'Jennifer is used to being the baby and the most precious member of the family——'

'Come off it, Georgie! Jennifer is grown up and has been for a long time now. She would have shouldered the responsibility of Celine easily enough. Celine could have done with her kind, gentle ways too. It was a risk bringing you in your sister's stead, but if you so much as touch that girl you'll have me to answer to. She needs loving, not bullying, and that's what she's going to get from both of us.'

Georgina sighed. 'How did her mother die?' she asked.

'In a fire. Celine was got out of the house by some neighbours, but they couldn't get her mother out. Celine's father tried to make the child talk it out of her system, but she wouldn't say a single word. Whenever he mentioned Alice, his wife, the child shut up like a clam with a dreamy look in her eyes, and she's been like that ever since.'

'Poor girl!'

William glanced at Georgina and it seemed as if a reflection of that fire was lighting his eyes. 'I'd give anything to make that girl happy,' he said abruptly. 'I owe it to her father—and the girl herself. She's beautiful, Georgie, the most beautiful creature I've ever seen.'

Georgina raised her eyebrows. 'More beautiful than Jennifer?'

'Good lord, yes! Jennifer has a fragile prettiness, but this girl is out of this world!'

'And you think Jennifer would have tolerated comparison

with a raving beauty?' Georgina was stung into asking. 'She'd have got rid of Celine somehow—especially if she knew how fond of her you are! Her gentle ways wouldn't have lasted two minutes after she realised she was expected to share your attention with somebody else. You've had a lucky escape, William, my lad!'

'By being stuck with you? Don't you ever have anything pleasant to say for your sister?'

Georgina bit her lip. 'I've known Jennifer all her life,' she reminded him. 'She doesn't share things—with anyone.'

'Only because she's had to put up with your petty jealousies whenever she wanted to strike out for herself. Older sisters can have one hell of a lot to answer for when they constantly resent being put in the shade by their younger siblings. Still, it's a risk I've chosen to take with Celine. You might say the choice was forced on me: either I got married to make a home for her, or I should have had to put her in a home and visit whenever I could. I chose to marry you—and I'll make it work if it's the last thing I do! You won't make Celine suffer for your inadequacies as you did Jennifer, my girl. I've got your measure, and if anyone can handle you, I can!'

Georgina bent her head. 'What will you do if Celine recovers? She may not stay a child for ever. Have you thought of that?'

'I can't afford to,' he dismissed the question. 'I have to think of her as a child. One can't think of her as anything else.'

But he already did, Georgina thought, surprised by the insight he had given her into his feelings. It had been Celine all the time! Was it possible? Could he really have decided to marry Jennifer for no other reason but that she would be kind to Celine? If so, where did she stand herself as Jennifer's substitute?

'A child in a woman's body,' she mused aloud. 'Does she know I'm coming?'

He nodded. 'I had her brought over from Australia last week. She's already installed in the house at Nuwara Eliya where we're staying while I'm working on this irrigation project.'

'Alone?' Georgina gasped.

'Of course not! She has her nurse with her—a woman I very much want to get rid of, incidentally. If you can do that for me, I'll be eternally in your debt.'

Georgina eyed him covertly. 'Are you afraid of this dragon? I don't believe it!'

'You needn't. Miss Campbell doesn't alarm me, she bores me with her baby-talk and her upsy-daisies! Celine doesn't understand much, but she's a human being and should be addressed as such.'

Georgina allowed herself a faint smile. 'All right,' she said, 'I'll get rid of your Miss Campbell for you. Anything to oblige and all that.'

His eyes narrowed, openly mocking her. 'Anything?'

'Almost anything,' she amended, and yawned to show she didn't care what he thought. But she did care! And she was alarmed too, because now she was back at the beginning with him, not knowing or understanding him at all. She had got used to his being in love with Jennifer. Now she didn't know if he was in love with anybody at all—and she had to know! She had to know *something*!

She cleared her throat, hesitated, and then started again in a now or never voice that betrayed her nervousness. 'William, why did you marry me? As an alternative Miss Campbell?'

'Does it matter?' He stood up, pushing back his chair with a vigour that had the backs of her hands tingling.

'It matters to me,' she said.

He bent over her, leaning his hands on the arms of her chair. 'Does it? Why did you marry me, Georgie Porgie? You see, you can't answer that either, can you? It's better not to ask questions that have no answer to them. It'll have to be enough for you that you're here—that in itself fulfils one of your ambitions, doesn't it? Haven't you always wanted to travel and see the world?'

'Yes,' she admitted. 'But I want to know where I stand too. Was all you wanted a nursemaid for Celine?'

His face was unreadable, at least to her. 'I wanted a wife. Wives are usually expected to share their husband's responsibilities, aren't they?'

She made a last effort to explain her anxieties to him. 'I don't resent Celine——'

'You haven't met her yet. You resented Jennifer all right and with much less cause. Where do you want to stand, Georgina?'

She shrugged her shoulders. 'I want adventure!' she burst out. 'I don't know what exactly!' Only she did. She wanted the whole of her adventuring to be with him! 'Are you in love with Celine?'

His fingers brushed her cheek. 'My dear girl, are you going to be jealous of her too? I don't kiss Celine like this—at least you can be sure of that!' He bent his head and put his lips to hers, kissing her hard and with an expertise that rendered her breathless and made her heart pound against her ribs. 'She won't be taking anything away from you, Georgie Porgie, and you'll fight with her at your peril! If you want to let fly at anyone, you'll have to make do with me. Okay?'

It was so unfair! But then she caught sight of the slight yellowing that was all that was left of the black eye she had given him and her conscience was aroused, making her feel both uncertain and tearful.

'I don't want to fight with anybody!' she exclaimed.

He straightened his back, looking down at her with amused eyes. 'That'll be the day, my dear. Come and eat. You'll be meeting Celine soon enough and then you can make up your own mind about her. The only thing that's wrong with your fighting instincts right now is that you're half asleep.' A smile flickered across his lips. 'Shall I carry you, or will you walk?'

She stood up quickly, avoiding his helping hand with a disdainful gesture. 'You'll never have to carry me, William Ayres!' she declared. 'I can look after myself, just as I always have!'

'But you have a husband now,' he reminded her. 'Won't you allow him to look after you?'

If she only could! 'A husband is as a husband does,' she answered pertly. 'I don't need a keeper too, you know, so you'd better keep your care for Celine—and Jennifer if you have any over. I'll pull my own weight, thank you very much!'

He stopped her with a touch of his hand. 'Not against me you won't, my love!' He pulled her close against him and kissed the tip of her nose with a mockery that made her want to cry. 'Little Miss Independence!' he added on a laugh.

# CHAPTER FIVE

The road to Kandy enchanted Georgina. She loved the changes in the scenery as they climbed further and further away from the sea. First there had been the coconut palms, their trunks weaving gorgeous patterns against the vivid blue sky; then there had been the paddy fields, some of them bright with water and some of them covered with the vivid green of the rice; and then, finally, there were the first of the tea plantations, hundreds of ruthlessly clipped back bushes marching their way across the higher slopes of the hill country, their lines keeping a military precision.

There were the changes in the people too. In an island noted for its beautiful women, most of them seemed to be out in the streets that morning, smiling and waving and dodging out of the way of the constantly hooting traffic as they went about their tasks of the day. The clutter of shops, single-storied and bursting at the seams with fruit and coconuts and other local commodities, came and went, giving way to long stretches of teak forest, rubber plants, and other crops. But it was the rice fields that appealed most of all to Georgina. To see the water-buffaloes doing their twice yearly task of ploughing the inundated mud of the terraced fields, their owners urging them on to greater effort, was for her symbolic of a whole way of life she would never have seen anywhere in the familiar world of the West. This was what she had dreamed would be the stuff of the intriguing East.

'Still want to go home?' William's voice cut across her contented thoughts.

She shook her head. 'No wonder they thought this must have been the Garden of Eden. Is it always so beautiful?'

'Probably. The Buddhist temples help the scene along, don't you think? The shape of those stupas must be one of the most satisfactory ever invented by man.'

Georgina followed where he was pointing to the domed buildings surmounted by a steeple, pencil-thin and narrowing towards the summit, and had to agree with him. 'Some of them are very old, aren't they?' she asked.

'Before we go home I'll take you to Anuradhapura and Polonnaruwa where you can see some really old ones. They were building these huge domes here when we in Europe were congratulating ourselves on managing a few arches. Originally, they were built over a relic of the Lord Buddha, or of one of his more renowned followers, together with the treasure given by whoever had had the temple built as an act of devotion. I can't believe there were enough relics to go round for all of them, however, but it doesn't matter, for Buddha and his teachings are brought to the mind whenever one sees a stupa, or dagoba, or pagoda, as we call it in England, after a while.'

'I'm surprised no one thought to steal the treasure,' Georgina remarked.

'I've never heard that they ever did,' William told her. 'I rather like to think the Buddhist philosophy precludes such reprehensible vices as greed and violence. Sometimes it does, and sometimes it doesn't.'

Georgina gave him a saucy look. 'I didn't know you had pacifist leanings. They don't show much, if you don't mind my saying so?'

'It takes two to make peace, just as it takes two to quarrel,' he observed. He grinned suddenly, taking her breath away. 'Besides, I shouldn't like my warrior wife to find it dull living with me. As far as you're concerned, my girl, I give as good as I get!'

It was strange to feel such a strong liking for her old enemy as she did now. 'I'm still one black eye to the good,' she reminded him. 'Perhaps it doesn't count,' she added, 'because I repented it almost at once. And it was partly your own fault. You practically dared me to hit you!'

'I can't say I thought you would,' he retorted dryly. 'You won't get through my defences as easily another time.'

'I may not want to hit you again,' she murmured.

'You will! *One little kiss*—that's all it takes with you, Georgie Porgie! But I'll tame you in the end. I'll have you eating out of my hand, a reformed character, you see if I don't!'

She was silent. Back in England she might have argued the point with him, mostly because she was afraid that she already liked the feeling of his hands on the reins far too well, but here it would have seemed strident and out of place to have denied the possibility that there might come a time when she wouldn't want to fight him—if that time wasn't already upon her.

*One little kiss!*

The memory of the brief kiss he had given her the evening before stirred her blood and she found herself speculating on her reactions if he should want more than a few kisses from her. The thought of it made her burn with an emotion she had never experienced before.

The Moslem women in the village they were passing through covered their heads with the loose folds of their saris, but they too were out in the street doing their shopping and standing in little groups exchanging the day's gossip. She felt very close to them. She felt very close to all women at that moment, for they too, some of them, had been caught up in the tide that held her in its grip for the first time in her life. They too knew what it was like to be submerged in a need for someone else—only why did it have to be *William*? How much easier life would be for her if she could have gone on hating him in peace!

'Kandy isn't far now. We'll stop there for lunch and go on to Nuwara Eliya afterwards,' he told her.

'Is that where you're going to be working?'

'Fairly near. I'll be able to get back most nights. I was fortunate to be offered the use of this house on one of the tea plantations there. It'll be more comfortable for you and Celine than anything the site will be able to offer.'

'I don't mind roughing it,' Georgina asserted. 'I don't want any favours from you!'

'You won't get many, but Celine deserves something better than the dust and grit of a dam in the building. Her father always gave her the best, and so shall I!'

Which meant that Georgina would be expected to do so too, she thought wryly. Oh well, it wouldn't be new to her to come second to someone else. What else had it ever been with Jennifer?

'Have you seen the house?' she asked, making conversation because she didn't want to be left to think her own thoughts an instant longer.

'No. I've only been to Sri Lanka once before and that was on a brief trip from a job I was doing in India. I thought I'd like to spend longer here, so I applied to help build this dam. I was very much interested in the historic aspects of their irrigation systems here. They're absolutely fantastic!—and built long before our modern machinery came along. I want to make a study of how they were done, to see what we can learn from it. It's a pity they were so neglected later on, but the European conquerors weren't interested in rice or the hinterland, they were attracted by the cinnamon and other spices and weren't any too nice in their methods of getting as much of the stuff as possible. The "bunds", as they call the dams here, and the "tanks", or artificial lakes, fell into disrepair and are only being put right now. At one time Ceylon fed twice the population she has now and still had rice over for exporting, now she has to import about a third of what she eats. It's getting better, but they still have a long way to go to catch up with their own history.'

'But surely nowadays——'

'Don't underrate the men of old,' he said dryly. 'We have the technology to do wonderful things nowadays, but have we the will? They lacked our machinery, but their deeds survive them to tell of their genius. We haven't yet built any comparable irrigation system in our time.'

Georgina was impressed. 'Was it very long ago?'

'I'm afraid it was. Europe had a long, long way to go in those days.'

Georgina made a face. 'I'm suitably chastened,' she said. 'Does it give you a good feeling to be treading in such august footsteps with your own project?'

He flushed absurdly, looking young and eager. 'It does, but I hadn't expected you to understand something like that. You're a much more complicated person than I thought!'

'Perhaps we all are,' she suggested. 'I mean, I don't think I know you very well either. I thought I did, but we're strangers really, aren't we? First impressions aren't always the most accurate after all. How I hated you that day!'

He laughed. 'It showed!' he said. 'You've been trying to hate me ever since, haven't you?'

'Not more than you despised me. And I still hate you! I hate you every moment of every day!'

He slowed the car, his eyes flicking to her face and back to the road. 'Who are you trying to convince, yourself or me?'

She clenched her fists and found one of them covered by his own, much larger hand. 'I don't know what you mean,' she declared. 'I don't have to convince anyone about that! Ask anyone!'

'Funnily enough, I did. I asked my mother.' His eyes flicked over her face again, noting the strain beneath her hardly won composure. 'Did you know she prefers you to your sister any day?'

'Yes.'

'Ah, but did you know why?'

She shook her head, not trusting herself to speak.

'She thinks you have courage. I hope you're not going to prove her wrong by continuing to insist you hate me, because you don't, do you, little Georgie? She doesn't think you ever have.'

Georgina chewed frantically on her lower lip. 'I don't like you!' she managed at last.

'Liking is a very pale emotion. It doesn't warm the blood—as I can warm yours any time I choose. *That's* something else!'

Georgina lifted her chin. 'Any attractive man could do the same! It doesn't mean anything. I don't think it's anything to congratulate yourself about. It—it doesn't make me like you any more!'

'Nevertheless,' he said with a smile she could only think would have done justice to the Bad Baron in a pantomime, 'it gives me a great deal of pleasure to know I have you at my mercy——'

She trembled. Was it possible he knew of the strange excitement that burned inside her whenever he came near? If he did, she would have to make it equally clear to him that she was ashamed of all such emotions. But how to do it?

'You're making far too much of very little! What makes you think I shall ever change my mind about you? I'll fight you to the last ditch! Just because you took me by surprise and—and *kissed* me, and I didn't *say* anything, it didn't mean I *liked* it!' She took a deep breath, preparing to hurry on with her castigations of his behaviour, but he seemed totally unperturbed. The hand that was covering hers patted her lightly on the knee.

'Took you by surprise? My dear girl, husbands are usually expected to kiss their wives. Indeed, the complaint is usually that they don't do it often enough!'

'In the normal way.' She cast him a glowering look. 'Ours isn't a normal marriage! Do you think I *want* to be kissed by someone who is obviously wishing I were somebody else? You should have put up more of a fight for Jennifer. Haven't you always thought of her as a nice, biddable girl? Well then, why didn't you make her change her mind about Duncan? She would have done if you'd pressed hard enough.'

His lips twitched. 'Somehow I prefer greater enthusiasm in my wife——'

'Then you shouldn't have married *me*!'

He grinned. 'But I did marry you, my dear, and now I'm looking forward to the rewards of having done so.'

She swallowed the lump in her throat, making a supreme effort to keep her voice light and airy. 'What makes you think I shall be any more loyal than Jennifer?' she taunted him. 'We are sisters, after all! And *I'm* not at all in love with you!'

His hand closed over hers, his fingers as hard as steel bands. 'Try it and see what happens to you. I'm not the type of man who competes for the favours of his wife, Georgina, and you are my wife, whether you like it or not.'

'Only because——'

'You can't argue your way out of this one, Mrs Ayres. You're caught in a snare of your own making when you said the words that made you a wife. *My* wife!'

'I didn't have much choice,' she protested, but there wasn't a great deal of conviction in her words. Nobody could have *made* her say the words, nobody but herself, so why had she?

'Your jealousy of Jennifer *made* you,' he countered dryly. 'You never count the cost when it comes to the long-standing rivalry between you! However, I'm not complaining. Haven't you promised me that you're better than she is?'

She flushed. 'I only meant——' She broke off, finding it impossible to discuss with him whether she or Jennifer had the better figure. When one was loved such things hardly mattered, and if one was not loved it mattered even less.

'Yes?'

'I'm not jealous of Jennifer!' she protested in a whisper. 'Why should I be? She hasn't anything I want and she never has had!'

'Not even the ability to attract every man in sight?' he put in dryly. 'When she was around nobody ever looked twice at you, did they, Georgie, not unless you forced yourself on their attention with your fists! Going away to college should have given you the space to find yourself. I wonder why it didn't. Away from your sister, you're not as strident as you are in her company. When you hold on to that temper of yours you're quite an attractive girl. Why didn't you take the opportunity to make your own friends?'

She uttered a mirthless laugh, hunching up her shoulders and refusing to answer. How could she tell him that most of the friends she had shared with Jennifer had been hers in the first place? He would never believe that it wasn't she, but Jennifer, who had resented her popularity and had done everything she could to subvert her friends to herself. Georgina had never cared sufficiently to bother about her sister's activities, but now she wished she had. She would have liked to have flung half a dozen potential lovers in William's face! It would have given her a most rewarding pleasure to have flicked her fingers at him and gone off with somebody else—somebody who would have more charm in his little finger than William had in his whole body, a fact she would have brought home to him with the kind of insolent derision to which he frequently treated her!

When the haze of tears cleared from her eyes she found the car had stopped and they were parked in the centre of a town whose buildings could only have been built by the British but which, nevertheless, was completely foreign to the English high streets it so closely emulated. Of course the people who thronged the pavements could never have been English. There were the men, spare and narrow-hipped in their sarongs, and the women as bright as butterflies in their distinctive saris if they were rich enough to wear such a costume; some of them seemed to have no more than a much washed skirt, similar to those worn by the men, and a bolero top that accentuated their very feminine figures.

'Never mind,' said William, 'you have me now.'

She jumped, wringing her hands together. 'What?'

'You may have few friends, but you've landed yourself a husband, Georgie Porgie.' He stroked her cheek with his forefinger. 'Wake up, Madam wife, this is Kandy. Are you hungry?'

She stared at him, not really seeing him at all. 'Really, William, how Victorian can you get? Madam wife, indeed!'

'Why not?' His smile forced a shiver up her spine. 'I have very Victorian ideas about marriage. He for God only; she for God in him! It goes with the decor the British Raj left behind!'

'That was in India,' she pointed out in husky tones. The shiver had settled into a space round her heart, increasing in intensity until she was afraid it would explode inside her. 'Yes, let's go and eat! And may we stop for a while and see the Temple of the Tooth? Is it genuinely a tooth from Buddha himself? I'd love to see that!'

'A whole lot safer than crossing swords with your husband?' he suggested, mocking her hurried, breathless speech.

'Not at all! I'm hungry!'

He shrugged his shoulders. 'Why not? The rest will keep until after you've met Celine.'

Georgina's spirits deflated with all the speed of a pricked balloon. *Celine!* How could she have forgotten all about her, even for a moment?

'I suppose Celine is your Victorian romantic dream?' she murmured, and then almost immediately, 'I shouldn't have said that. I'm sorry—only you did ask for me to say something nasty. You seem to enjoy getting me all riled up about nothing at all.'

He studied her closely and she could feel herself colouring angrily under his regard. 'I like to have my first impressions confirmed. They're not as inaccurate as you would like me to believe, my Georgie Porgie! You never miss an opportunity to rise and snap, do you? But be careful! There's a hook in the bait when you play such games with me. I always play to win and, unlike the Duncans of this world, I never, never cry!'

'You may do one day,' she muttered, put out. 'Everyone cries sometimes!'

His eyes narrowed. 'I shouldn't bet on it.'

She would have liked to have turned away and have talked about something else—anything, as long as it didn't mean they had to go on fighting. But she was far too stubborn to allow him to see she was worsted.

'Are you as nasty to poor Celine too?' she asked him, looking him straight in the eyes.

'You'll have to judge for yourself,' he said, and added, 'Celine doesn't answer back. She's all woman in that way, having learned that more victories are won with soft words by the fair sex. Why don't you try it some time?'

'I wouldn't be so patronising!'

He placed a finger across her lips, effectively silencing her. 'Is that what it is? My, my, but you tempt me to teach you better! *All* is fair in love and war, my dear.'

'And which is it in Celine's case?' she demanded, resisting the temptation to bite his finger. 'I already know which it is with me!'

'Do you? I wonder?' He reached into the car for his coat and shut and locked the doors. 'Come along and we'll eat! I'd like to show you the Temple today, Georgie, but we haven't any time to spare if we're to get to Nuwara Eliya before dark.'

Georgina was unbearably disappointed. 'Does it matter?' she pleaded.

He nodded. 'It's raining in the hills and that may delay us considerably as it is. I'm sorry, my dear, but there'll be other times.'

But she wouldn't be alone with him then, she thought, and wondered why it should be so important to her that she should have his full attention all to herself. She gave in with a good grace, however, accepting the inevitable with a gallant smile that he found touching in its insouciance. It was a little surprising too, he reflected, for he had always been led to believe that Georgina would bear a grudge for years, sulking over what everyone else had long forgotten. But this Georgina had courage, as his mother had suggested, and scorned to fight with weapons others might well have seized upon, fair or not. This Georgina had a tough, honest quality that he found he admired almost as much as it amused him.

They had lunch at a small local restaurant overlooking the lake which lends an air of enchantment to the whole city. William advised Georgina to follow his example and eat one of the curries that had pride of place on the menu. Georgina, who had a taste for hot, spicy foods, agreed readily and was delighted with the result. Half a dozen dishes were brought to their table, some of them familiar and some of them not, and she had an extremely agreeable half-hour tasting them all one by one.

William eyed her with a tolerant air. 'I don't believe it's even occurred to you that you might upset your tummy with all this strange food,' he observed.

'Why should it?'

'It has been known to. A change of germs more than a change of food probably, but the results are the same.'

'Pooh,' said Georgina. 'A few germs? I won't allow them to get the better of me! I'm enjoying myself far too much!'

'I hope you're right,' he said dryly.

The rain had already started when they left the restaurant. It was more low cloud that had got trapped between the hills than actual rain, but there was a distinct dampness in the air and the sun had completely disappeared for the day.

'It's still beautiful even in the rain,' Georgina sighed, turning round in her seat to see the last of Kandy. 'Did you see those gorgeous flowering trees? The university campus is full of them! I've never seen anything like it!'

'The mauve ones are jacaranda, the scarlet flamboyant—no, that one is a flame tree, I think. The pink ones are new to me too.'

'And the bushes?' she asked eagerly.

'Bougainvillea. I can remember a time when they trailed over things, but they seem to have got them to stand up by themselves nowadays, and to come in so many colours that they're a feast to the eyes all by themselves.' He pointed with a finger at another, darker tree in the middle distance. 'There's an ebony tree.'

Georgina sat back, contented. 'It was worth coming just to see the flowers and the paddy fields and—and everything,' she said.

'But it would be better still without me?'

Georgina was surprised by the question. She averted her face and stared out at the grey drizzle. 'No, you make a good guide,' she said grudgingly. 'I wouldn't have known what anything was by myself.'

'A good book could have told you.'

She moved uncomfortably. 'I never recognise flowers and birds in books. They always look different somehow.'

He grimaced at the wet road ahead. 'Well, thank you for that recommendation at least,' he drawled. 'It doesn't say much for my personal qualities though, does it?'

'You don't think much of mine,' she retorted.

The rain grew steadily heavier as they climbed higher. It was strange to see the heavy grey skies dominating the countryside that always, in pictures, was bathed in eternal sunshine. The hairpin bends became more and more slippery too, demanding William's total concentration. Georgina was glad of the silence. She had thought the lower slopes spectacular, but the higher they went, the more beautiful it became. There were waterfalls everywhere and glistening white stupas of Buddhist temples hidden away in unexpected valleys. Sometimes, too, the heavily carved square towers that tapered inwards towards the top that marked the Hindu temples rose above the simple buildings of the villages, lending an exotic touch in contrast to the down-at-heel squalor of these high country villages. The Tamil workers, imported from South India for the backbreaking endless task of picking the tea, were the poorest people in the land, and it showed.

The tea factories were the largest buildings to be seen now. They all looked much the same, several stories high, with square, impersonal windows that gazed out across the miles of tea which surrounded them. Sometimes a plume of smoke rose from an asbestos pipe that served as a chimney, but on this wet, gloomy day few of the factories were working as hardly any tea had been picked.

'They'll be glad of the rain all the same,' William said with satisfaction. 'It's been a very dry wet season and tea needs a certain amount of moisture to flourish as it should.' He went on to explain that the higher it grew the finer was the tea obtained. 'But you'll find out all about that for yourself once you're settled in. Some of the best tea in the world is produced on the plantation where we're living.'

Georgina looked at the green bushes with renewed interest. It was funny how one took things for granted, she thought, recollecting the number of times she had made the tea at home without ever giving a thought as to how it was grown and prepared before it arrived on the shelf of the nearby supermarket.

'Jennifer doesn't like tea,' she said, apropos of nothing.

William favoured her with a blank stare. 'Jennifer isn't here to dislike it right now. Can't you leave her where she is, at home in England?'

Georgina pulled in her lower lip, looking away from him. 'Can you?'

'Easily.' He changed down to negotiate a particularly awkward corner. 'Have a look at the map, will you? I think we're nearly there.'

Georgina did as she was told, but the criss-crossing black lines on the plain white paper seemed to bear little relation to the road they were on.

'It's so smudged,' she said, 'it's impossible to tell where we are. Is this the best map you've got?'

'The only one.' He stopped the car and took it from her, huffing and puffing over the almost illegible names. 'Not much help, is it?'

Georgina pointed hopefully ahead. 'Let's go on and hope for a signpost,' she suggested.

He shrugged, putting the map back on her knee. 'We'll try it,' he agreed.

They rounded the next corner to be faced by a very English scarlet letter-box, bearing the insignia of Queen Victoria. There was nothing else, not so much as a single house, anywhere near it. William got out of the car, pulling his collar up against the rain, and went to take a closer look at it. He came back almost immediately.

'We're here,' he announced. 'I reckon the entrance must be just along the road.'

And so it proved. A tree-lined earth road led several miles through the tea gardens, went past a Hindu temple made of corrugated iron down below, but with a truly handsome painted and elaborately carved tower that marked it unmistakably for what it was. Beyond were the lines, where the Tamil workers lived. To Georgina's relief they seemed to be better housed on this estate than most of the others they had seen. And then, when they were least expecting it, the grey stone house, set in a charming English-style garden, came into sight and a few moments later they were drawing up outside the porch that sheltered the front door.

The doors were flung open and a servant came out with an umbrella to usher them into the house.

'Tea is waiting for you in the drawing-room, sir, madam,' he murmured to them. 'The two ladies are waiting for you there.'

Georgina hung back, regretting the loss of the intimacy of the interior of the car. Here, in a strange house among strange people, would she ever have William to herself again? But even as she was wishing herself back on the rain-sodden road, a young girl every bit as fair as Jennifer but much, much more beautiful came rushing across the polished floor and flung herself into William's arms.

'Darling William, this is some bungalow!' She kissed him warmly, arching her body against his as a cat does when it winds itself about one's legs. 'I thought you were never coming! Am I still the prettiest girl you know?' This last was said in such soft, seductive tones that Georgina blushed for her.

'You're still the most beautiful by far!' William answered, laughing. 'Now, calm down and say hullo to Georgina, minx.'

Celine looked straight through Georgina, her eyes completely blank. 'Who is she? Why did you have to bring her here, William?'

William patted the girl's shoulder, a great sadness crossing his face.

'Georgina is my wife,' he said.

# CHAPTER SIX

Miss Campbell was tall and statuesque with one of the ugliest faces Georgina had ever seen. It wasn't any particular feature that ruined her looks, but an unfortunate combination of them all, coupled with a colouring that was sallow to the point of being yellow.

She remained seated as the party moved into the drawing-room from the hall. Indeed, she barely looked up as they entered, preferring to continue a rather high-pitched conversation with the only other occupant of the room, a young man who was standing behind the comfortable sofa on which she was sitting, nursing a cup of tea.

'You underrate her understanding,' he was saying angrily.

'Do I?' Miss Campbell rejoined. 'Then what am I doing here?'

'I've been wondering that ever since you both arrived.' His tea-cup rattled precariously as he changed it from one hand to the other. 'You never let her out of your sight!'

'That's what Miss Campbell is paid for,' William said dryly from the doorway. 'You are speaking of Celine, I take it?'

The young man stood his ground. 'She's not a child! Why discuss her as if she were?' He looked from William to Georgina. 'Is this another gaoler for her?'

'I hope not!' Georgina exclaimed.

The young man managed a smile. 'I'm sorry,' he said, 'but it makes me angry to see wild animals confined in cages.'

Celine appeared pleased by this. 'Am I a wild animal?' she demanded eagerly. 'Stuart, am I?'

81

The young man tousled her hair. 'A very beautiful one!'

'Wild animals are dangerous!'

He grinned at her. 'Are you dangerous?'

Celine lowered her lashes, peeping at him through them. 'Not with you, darling Stuart. *Never* with you!'

William cut her off with a brusqueness that Georgina thought both unnecessary and unkind. 'Celine, behave yourself! I don't want to forbid Stuart to come to the house——'

'What nonsense!' Georgina put in hastily. She moved closer to Stuart herself. 'I'm Georgina Perry,' she said, holding out her hand to him.

He shook it gravely. 'Mrs Ayres,' he corrected her, amused by the slip. 'My name is Stuart Duffield. I work here on the estate.'

'He's the most important person here!' Celine claimed. 'They couldn't do anything without him!'

Georgina raised her brows in silent enquiry and the young man laughed. 'I'm the fellow who tastes the tea,' he explained. 'Every estate has one who makes sure that the tea doesn't undergo any process for too long, thus spoiling it. It's a bit like wine tasting. They'll be getting a local chap in to do my job before long, but meanwhile, I enjoy it here. The manager is a good friend of mine. You must meet him and his wife as soon as I can arrange it. His name is Peter, Peter Kotalawala.'

'He has an English name because he's a Catholic,' Celine chimed in. 'His wife is sweet!'

'Only because she allows you to do as you like,' Miss Campbell said with menace. 'She has no control over you at all!'

'She's not my keeper. She's not a spoilsport either.' Celine turned a blank stare on Georgina. 'What are you?'

Georgina opened her mouth to answer, but William did it for her. 'She's my wife,' he said.

'And too pretty to be a spoilsport,' Stuart added.

'She's not as beautiful as I am!' Celine spat at him, annoyed.

'No one could be that,' he agreed cheerfully. 'But beauty isn't everything, duckie. Georgina is very much my type!' He flashed a meaning look at the surprised Georgina. 'Pity she's already taken!'

Celine was furious. 'You mean you prefer Georgina to me?' she demanded.

'It's a different thing. You can't compare the two. You're my friend; Georgina—well, she could be something else!'

Georgina swallowed hard, not daring to look in William's direction. 'No, she couldn't be!' she stammered out. 'I couldn't!'

To her surprise William laughed. 'You're embarrassing my wife,' he said wryly to Stuart. 'She isn't accustomed to compliments from the opposite sex. You'll have to go easily with her.'

Georgina could have stamped her foot with sheer, unreasoning rage. Did he have to make it so blatant that she had no attraction for him? And how could one deny such a slight? She couldn't insist that she had had her share of compliments without sounding a boastful fool, and yet it hurt to let his disparagement go by as if it meant nothing to her. The trouble was that she wanted William's regard, wanted it badly, and was in danger of getting everything else out of perspective in consequence.

Happily, Stuart shook his head in stunned disbelief. 'What's wrong with the men back home?' he wondered.

Georgina forced a wavering smile. 'I have a sister——'

'And she takes everyone's eye?' Stuart whistled in derision. 'She didn't take your husband's, did she, or you wouldn't be here!'

Georgina's heightened colour and obvious distress was an answer in itself. She saw the baffled expression on Stuart's face and wished the ground would open and swallow her up before she was forced to hear William's rejoinder. Would he admit that she was only his wife as second best?

'Jennifer has the looks, Georgina the character,' William said steadily.

'I wish more people thought that way,' Miss Campbell approved. 'But there, most people waste their time spoiling the beautiful while we plainer mortals have to make do with the crumbs. Mrs Ayres is lucky to have found a perceptive man who doesn't think beauty is everything——'

'Am I so ugly?' Georgina burst out.

'Not in my book!' Stuart replied promptly. 'Some kinds of beauty are extraordinarily dull, and you would never be that! Give me warmth and generosity any time!' He bowed with a play-acting formality to Georgina, his hand on his heart. 'You're my ideal woman, Mrs Ayres. Call on me any time!'

She made him a curtsey. 'Thank you, Mr Duffield, I'll bear it in mind.'

'You'll do nothing of the sort!' William's anger was as unexpected as it was forceful. 'Shall we change the subject before one of us says something we'll regret? Perhaps you, Miss Campbell, would be good enough to show my wife round the bungalow. You stay here, Celine. I want to talk to you!'

Celine smiled sunnily up at him. 'I want to go with Georgie! Stuart isn't the only one who likes her—I like her too. *She* won't make me do things I don't want to do!'

'I shouldn't be too sure of that,' William retorted.

Georgina held her head high. 'My husband thinks I'm a bully too,' she said to no one in particular. 'I think it's because I succeeded in giving him a black eye not long ago. You can still see the remains of it if you look carefully.'

It was Stuart who laughed. 'A nice plush one! What a girl!'

William grinned reluctantly. 'She won't do it again. We have better things to do nowadays.'

What a pity he didn't mean it, Georgina thought, and

wondered why it should hurt so much that he didn't. She smothered a sigh and turned to Miss Campbell, whose look of pure hatred caught her unawares. Why? she wondered. Why should Miss Campbell dislike her with such intensity?

'Come this way, Mrs Ayres,' the older woman bade her. 'We've prepared the master suite for you and your husband. It looks over the garden with the tea gardens in the distance. I hope you'll like it.'

Georgina was astonished by the magnificence of the house. To call such a dwelling a bungalow seemed to her to verge on the ridiculous. Each of the bedrooms she glanced into was spacious and beautifully fitted out, but the master suite was out of this world. There were two bedrooms, one feminine and flouncy, the other decorated with a more masculine restraint, joined together by a bathroom full of solid, Edwardian equipment such as she had never seen before.

'The water doesn't often get hot,' Miss Campbell sniffed, 'and, as you can see, the roof leaks, but I suppose one can't expect anything else so far from civilisation. Seeing that you're practically on your honeymoon, I don't suppose you'll notice our inconveniences, but I'm used to something better, I can tell you. I've given up a great deal to stay with Celine, poor child! I knew her father very well, but I suppose Mr Ayres will have told you all about that?'

Georgina frowned. 'No, he hasn't said much. What a lovely place this is! What about Celine's father?'

'I was called his housekeeper, but of course, I was much more than that. It was a tragedy when he died.'

'It must have been.' Georgina sat down on the edge of the bed. 'Did you know Celine's mother?' she asked.

Miss Campbell went a mottled red. 'That bitch? Celine takes after her. She hadn't a moral to her name!'

Georgina froze her with a look. 'Nevertheless, she was married to Celine's father and you—were not.'

'If you care to put it that way. He was well rid of her!'

Georgina looked down at her shoes. 'Were you in the fire too?'

'I got out. I was lucky. Celine was got out too.'

'But her mother died.'

Miss Campbell shrugged. 'I wasn't going back inside for her. She deserved to die.'

'No one deserves to die in a fire like that,' Georgina said gently. 'Miss Campbell, are you sure you're the right person to care for the daughter of someone you hated so much? It must be difficult to be constantly seeing her mother in Celine.'

'It doesn't matter with Celine. The child's simple, or hadn't you noticed? No man will ever make the mistake of marrying her!'

'I hope you're wrong, Miss Campbell. Meanwhile I have nothing to do with my time and I rather want to look after Celine myself. I imagine you could get another job quite easily?'

'You're asking me to go?'

Georgina looked her straight in the eyes. 'I'm telling you to go, Miss Campbell. Shall we say a month's notice and an extra month's pay at the end of that to tide you over until you find something else?'

Miss Campbell made a strangled sound. 'We'll see what Mr Ayres has to say about that! You won't get rid of me so easily, my fine madam! You'll never get rid of me!'

'We'll see.' Georgina crossed her fingers surreptitiously, praying that William would back her up and insist that the woman went. He had said he wanted to be rid of her, but not, perhaps, the minute of their arrival.

'You'll have to persuade Celine too,' Miss Campbell said, her twisted smile more confident. 'You've yet to see her in one of her states. It isn't a pretty sight and I very much doubt if you could cope with her single-handed as I've been expected to do these last years. We shall see, Mrs Ayres, whether I go or not after you've had to put up with her screaming for hours together. We'll see if you change your mind then!'

Georgina could only think how much she disliked this ugly woman. 'I shan't.'

Miss Campbell tossed her head. 'Very sure of ourselves, aren't we? Well, you won't find Mr Ayres at all pleased by this day's work, young lady. *He* knows my value and remunerates me accordingly, and *I* didn't have to put myself out to attract him either! What did you offer him? A young, nubile body——'

'And a black eye,' Georgina muttered under her breath.

A look of venom crossed Miss Campbell's face. 'Poor Georgie Porgie, did she hope to wear the trousers and did she get a shock when she found her William has a mind of his own?'

'No, Miss Campbell, I did not. I've known William since I was ten years old, so I think I may be said to know exactly what he's like. Nor do I relish being called Georgie Porgie——'

'*He* calls you that!'

'He has privileges I don't accord to anyone else!' Georgina snapped. She felt both exasperated and weary. 'Please go away!'

'Very well, Mrs Ayres, but I shall be speaking to *Mr* Ayres about this, you may be sure!'

'About what?' William asked, coming into the bedroom through the bathroom door.

Absurdly, Georgina felt guilty at the sight of him. 'It doesn't matter now,' she began.

Miss Campbell folded her hands across her stomach, bridling with displeasure. 'Your—*wife* has taken it upon herself to give me notice, sir. She seems to think she can manage Celine all by herself! She has also been unpardonably rude, but I can hardly expect you to defend me from that now, can I? A strong-minded young lady, if you don't mind my saying so! She'd have us all bending to that will of hers if we allowed it, and that's the last thing Celine needs, as you very well know. I may be exceeding my duties, sir, but I will not have that poor girl bullied—not while I'm still in charge of her welfare!'

William's face froze. 'She won't be, Miss Campbell. I will see to that. Please leave us alone now, will you?'

'Of course, sir. But I should like to know whether I am to be dismissed or not? Mrs Ayres——'

'The decision is mine, Miss Campbell. It's true I've been thinking Celine might benefit from being treated more like anyone else than is possible when she is in the constant care of one used to very young children, but I've yet to make up my mind as to what future arrangements I shall be making for her. I'll let you know.'

'Yes, sir. Thank you, sir.'

Georgina made a face at her departing back. 'Three bags full, sir!'

'*Georgina!* I warned you——'

'You said you wanted to be rid of her!'

'Not if you're going to bully Celine in her stead. I won't have it, Georgie. What have you been saying to that woman?'

Georgina checked the hot words that threatened to pour from her. Losing her temper would not help her now. She spread her hands, wishing she were less vulnerable to his opinion of her.

'I gave her a month's notice. Apparently she doesn't think I have the right to employ whom I please in my own household, but I thought you'd back me up over this at least! She's a horrible woman and can't be doing Celine any good. Nor was I rude to her—not until she called me Georgie Porgie. I won't stand for that!'

'Was that all?' She could tell he didn't believe her and she was doubly hurt that he should prefer the word of that dragon of a woman. 'It wasn't, was it?'

Georgina sighed. 'She said Celine has crying fits when

she screams for hours together. But why does she have them, William? There must be some reason for her to behave like that. She was sunny enough when we arrived just now.'

'Hmm. She didn't like it when Stuart obviously preferred yourself to her.'

'Oh, that.' Georgina dismissed Stuart Duffield with an airy wave. 'She knew he wasn't serious. With her looks, she'll never have to worry about competition in that department!'

'She's too young in herself to worry about things like that,' William answered. 'Thank goodness that she is! We've problems enough without her getting ideas about boyfriends or marriage!'

'Why shouldn't she?' Georgina asked. 'Her body is quite grown up and there doesn't seem to be all that wrong with her mind. If she talks like a child, couldn't that be having to live with that impossible Miss Campbell?'

William put his hands on his hips and glared at her. 'D'you think you can do better?'

Georgina nodded. She pressed her lips together and straightened her shoulders. 'I'd like to try.'

Exasperation gave way to a more hopeful expression. 'Yes, but, Georgie, it won't do to bully her. You have to admit that Miss Campbell was pretty quick to sum you up. Celine wants a more gentle touch than yours. Jennifer——'

'Jennifer isn't here and I am! I think I can make Celine like me—I think she does already!—and I can't think Miss Campbell is the answer to anything. Where did Celine's father find her?'

'She found him. She's the old retainer type, devoted and selfless, though I have to admit I find her rather trying too.'

Georgina slanted a look up at him. 'I think she was in love with him,' she hazarded. 'She certainly hated Celine's mother.'

'Rubbish, my dear. The Miss Campbells of this world can't afford the luxury of falling in love with their employers. They know nothing will come of it.'

'Knowing doesn't always have the desired effect,' Georgina remarked wryly. Knowing that William was in love with Jennifer hadn't stopped her falling for him. Hope could survive on very little encouragement, or even none at all. 'William, I know my opinion doesn't count for much, but she was telling me about Celine's mother's death. She was in that fire too, but she didn't go back for that poor woman. Perhaps the fire was already too bad, but supposing it wasn't. I wouldn't put it past her to have stood by and watched her rival die.' She shuddered. 'Worse still, she says Celine is just like her mother. If she hated the mother so much, how does she feel about the daughter?'

William sat down on the bed beside her. 'My dear little Georgie, how your imagination runs away with you! What do you want me to do? Tell the old harridan to go? Celine can be quite a responsibility, you know. She has frequent nightmares and she can be spiteful if you cross her. Are you sure you want to take on all that single-handed?'

Georgina looked at him, her eyes pleading for something she thought he didn't have it in him to give. 'If I have your support,' she said. 'I thought you'd back me up with Miss Campbell, but you didn't. Okay, I know you don't trust me not to impose my ideas on other people, but you owe it to me to pretend we're a team in public. Or is that too much to ask?'

William's face softened. 'I can't afford to make a mistake, Georgie, not with someone as helpless as Celine. But I promise you, I'll back you all the way for as long as you restrain your tendencies to play the bully. Play fair with me and I'll play fair with you, but if you once try to manipulate that girl to suit yourself, I'll take you apart, piece by piece! Try a little feminine gentleness and see what wonders that works for you!'

'Try leaving me alone and see what that does!' she snapped back.

His expression changed to one of amusement. 'But I have no intention of leaving you alone, my pet. *That's* what I came in here to talk to you about.' He studied the stubborn lines of her face for a moment. 'Aren't you interested?' he enquired.

'Should I be?'

'Most brides are.'

'But I'm not most brides! And I'm not Jennifer—I'm *me*!'

His amusement increased. 'You're you and you won't change, is that it?'

'People don't change much,' she sighed, 'and you won't allow me to change the image you have of me, not that I care what you think! You always were prejudiced against me.'

His eyebrows rose. 'Was I?' He leaned closer. 'Shall we call a truce until we've settled down into being man and wife?'

'You never play fair!' she complained.

'A truce,' he said dryly, 'binds both parties, Georgie Porgie. Come on, love, give a little bit! I don't want to have you in tears every time I kiss you, and I mean to kiss you frequently in the near future. You are my wife after all.'

'You don't have to remind me of that! What a prize—to be the despised wife of Mr William Ayres, the man who's never wrong about anything! Well, you can take whatever you feel you have a right to, but if I want to cry, I'll cry all the time, and *you* won't be able to stop me!'

'It sounds like a lachrymose evening,' he drawled. He rolled away from her across the bed and went across the room to stare out of the window. 'You can always try and make me cry instead?' he invited her.

'That'll be the day! You don't care a toss what I do, or how I feel. You never have!'

He turned quickly. 'Should I be shedding tears over your fate, my Georgie? Are your tears shed for me rather than for yourself?'

She didn't know how to answer. She made a gesture of defeat. 'I don't expect love, but you're not even kind! Nor do I think making love should be reduced to a legal obligation.'

'Good lord!' he exclaimed. 'What do you expect? Bells ringing and violins playing off stage? Surely you, with your vast experience, must know it just doesn't happen like that?'

She ignored his sarcasm, wishing she had a small part of the experience he credited her with. 'Perhaps you've never had the right partner,' she struck out at him. She cowered away from the glint in his eyes, wishing herself anywhere else but there. 'If you had, you wouldn't behave as though it were nothing more than sharing a cup of tea!'

'Well, if one's wife isn't the right partner, who is?' he demanded softly, advancing towards her with such steely purpose that she shivered despite herself.

'One's beloved,' she insisted.

He came to a stop in front of her, their knees touching, and looked down at her, his eyes burning a deep gold. He was even larger than she had remembered, standing over her like that, and he looked more than capable of holding his own in any battle with her. Not that she would be putting up much of a fight, for she had never felt more weak and feminine, with a tingling fear that might have been mistaken for joyful anticipation of the coming struggle. Was it possible that she wanted to lose to him?

'William, we have to go back to the others! Please don't! *Not now!*'

'Why not now?' He sounded triumphant and very much in control of the situation.

'I'm not ready——' By contrast her own voice was ragged and unsteady. 'I'm tired and—and I'm hungry too.'

'Are you now?' He swept her up on to her feet and into the circle of his arms. She looked up at him fearfully and was astonished to find he was smiling. 'You seem smaller than ever. You fight like a heavyweight, so it comes as a constant surprise to find you such a small handful!'

'I haven't any shoes on,' she found herself explaining, 'and I stopped growing a long, long time ago, so I doubt I'll grow any larger——'

'I expect I'll get used to it in time,' he mocked her. His hand went to the collar of her dress and trailed an intimate line down to the hollow between her breasts. He unbuttoned the first button, and then another, ignoring her hesitant attempts to prevent him. 'Where's all that experience you were boasting about now?'

She clenched her fists, battering them against his chest. The blows wouldn't have hurt a fly and despair mingled with a burgeoning excitement that threatened to betray her into openly inviting his caresses. Even so, she was unprepared for the moment when he bent his head and his lips claimed hers with a force that made her glad of the strength of the arm that held her close up against him. She made a last, feeble protest before flinging her arms round his neck with an abandonment that would have shocked her to the core at any other time.

The harsh urgency of his kisses bewildered her as much as her own response, awakened new emotions she had never known existed inside her. When he pushed her gently back on to the bed, she clung to him as if her life depended on it.

'Don't go!' she flung at him. She buried her fingers into the hair at the nape of his neck and arched her body invitingly against his.

'I'm not going anywhere, my sweet.' He stripped off his shirt in a single movement and took her back into his arms. 'I want my wife and, it would seem, she wants me too! I can't say I believed I'd ever think you lovelier than Jennifer, but you have a beautiful body.' His mouth travelled from her lips to her breasts and back again, smiling deep into her eyes. 'Aren't you going to kiss me too?'

She shook her head. 'I can't.'

She felt his laughter rather than heard it. 'All those claims, my dear little Georgina, and you're as innocent as a young girl. Confess, you've never felt like this before, have you?'

She shook her head again. 'I've never——'

He turned her face gently towards his, exploring her mouth with his own. 'Never? Oh, Georgina! Why didn't you say so before?'

'You didn't ask me.'

He leaned up on his elbow, smoothing her hair away from her face. 'I still mean to have you, Georgie Porgie. I'll be as gentle as I can——'

His words were cut off by a yell of anguish from some other part of the bungalow. It came again and again, rending the air with its piteous sound.

'Celine!'

Georgina felt cold with shock. 'Celine? But it doesn't sound human! William, why?'

He pushed her away from him. 'How should I know? I'd better go to her. Sometimes, if one gets in early enough, one can stop her before she really gets started. You'd better get dressed too.'

Georgina pulled her clothes together with a heightened colour. 'If I'm going to look after her, I ought to go to her now,' she insisted. 'Poor girl! She sounds as though she's having a terrible nightmare, as if she's really asleep. I wish we could wake her up!'

'To her it's a nightmare, a nightmare of fire and death, but she won't talk about it. She never has.'

They went together to Celine's private sitting-room, where the girl sat for long hours on her own, refusing any company or occupation, preferring to spend her time staring with unseeing eyes into space. Now she was struggling to get away from Miss Campbell, who was attempting to calm her.

'I won't! I won't!' she was screaming. 'I won't tell them anything!'

Miss Campbell looked grim. 'Who would believe such nonsense? No one has ever seen a demon a hundred and twenty feet high, you stupid girl! Certainly not one with the head of a bear! I never heard such nonsense!'

'It was there!' roared Celine. 'I saw it! It had a thing like an elephant in its hand—an elephant-shaped cup! And then there was the fire again!'

Georgina pushed Miss Campbell to one side, taking the girl into her own arms. 'Shall we look for this demon together?' she asked her, hugging her tight. 'It's all right, Celine. I believe you!'

'It won't be there now,' Celine sobbed. 'It never is. Before, it was something else, but now it wears a mask and it drinks blood. I couldn't have imagined that, could I?'

'No,' said Georgina carefully, 'I don't think you could.'

Celine stopped yelling, amazed by this reaction. 'Nobody ever believed me before!' she sobbed. 'Never! Never! Only I've never seen a demon like this one before. He was *horrible*!'

Georgina's eyes met her husband's. 'William will find out his name and, when you know who he is, you won't be afraid of him any longer,' she promised soothingly. 'I'm sure he has a name.'

'They never have names!' Miss Campbell snapped.

'The first one did,' William remembered, sounding surprised himself. 'The first one was an Aborigine character.'

Miss Campbell sniffed. 'She shouldn't be encouraged in her fancies, sir. If you ask me, she frightens herself deliberately. I've no sympathy with her!'

'So I've noticed, Miss Campbell,' William returned smoothly. 'Happily, it seems that my wife has. Shall we leave her to finish calming Celine by herself? We would be better employed discussing the terms of your notice, I believe.'

Miss Campbell turned venomous eyes on to Georgina's startled face. 'You'll regret it!' she spat out. 'You'll both regret it!'

# CHAPTER SEVEN

The atmosphere at dinner was decidedly frosty. Georgina tried to tell herself that the depression was centred on Miss Campbell, but it was finally borne in on her that Miss Campbell was completely herself again, as was Celine, and the only person who seemed to be suffering from reaction after the scenes of a couple of hours earlier was herself.

She did her best to respond to Celine's overtures of friendship, but all she really wanted to do was to escape from the lot of them, to shut herself in her room and to howl herself to sleep.

'What are those masks in the hall?' she asked the girl—unwisely, she thought, the second the words had left her mouth.

'There's a whole craft industry centred round them in Sri Lanka,' Celine told her shyly. 'Do you like them?'

Georgina wondered how to answer. 'They're very colourful,' she said guardedly.

'I like them,' Celine volunteered. 'I like the small ones and the ones that don't move. They're different from—from——' Her mouth quivered and she looked fearfully across the table at Miss Campbell.

'Madam shouldn't have reminded you,' Miss Campbell reproached Georgina. 'Now, now, chicken! You don't want to water down your soup with your tears, do you? You get on with your food, my dear, and forget all about your little adventure. We don't want you having nightmares in the night, do we?'

The blankness came back into Celine's eyes. 'The moon is getting full now,' she said.

'That's right, dear. *Girls and boys, come out to play, The moon doth shine as bright as day!*'

A brand new suspicion crossed Georgina's mind. She turned impulsively towards her husband. 'Did you know Miss Campbell when you were fifteen?' she demanded.

His lips twitched. 'No, that was my own inspiration,' he answered. 'It was a long time ago, Georgie. Isn't it time you forgave me for that?'

'Never!' She glared at him, but a little giggle inside her betrayed her. 'It wasn't funny, William. It wasn't at all funny for me!'

'You made far too much of it—then and now.'

'*You* didn't have to listen to that dreadful rhyme being whispered by all and sundry every time you appeared anywhere. It hurt badly for years and years, especially as I was only trying to defend Jennifer from that little creep. It hurt terribly! I'd liked you up until that moment, you see, and then that had to happen!'

'My dear girl, you didn't like me at all! You were as prickly as a hedgehog.'

'I was ten years old.'

He smiled slowly. 'Is that an explanation or an excuse?'

She smiled too. 'You were so large. It never occurred to me that you might be feeling out of place at a children's party. All I was thinking about was how much I hoped you'd like me! You had a beautiful bicycle and I wanted to go for a ride on it. I thought you might take me upon the crossbar——'

'I invited you for a ride later on,' he reminded her. 'You refused.'

She flushed, looking young enough to be ten years old all over again. 'I had to refuse! I didn't want to have anything to do with you after—after coming out with *that*!'

'It could have been worse, my dear. I might have said: *There was a little girl who had a little curl, Right in the middle of her forehead. When she was good, she was very,*

*very good, But when she was bad, she was horrid!'*

'That wouldn't have done the same damage,' Georgina said at once. 'I wouldn't have minded that half so much.'

'Why not?' he asked, intrigued.

'That could have been anyone, the other one everyone knew to be me!'

He shrugged, losing interest. 'You do have a little curl, though. You had it then, and you have it now. Mother used to refer to it as your "kiss-curl". You have pretty hair, Georgie Porgie, even if it does lead a life of its own. It never stays put like Jennie's does.'

Georgina could have told him that she didn't use hair lacquer as her sister did, but she didn't. She sighed instead, wondering rather bleakly if there would ever come a time when he would cease to compare her with Jennifer all the time. She glanced out of the window at the steadily falling rain and took consolation from the thought that her sister would have hated everything about the bungalow and the sodden scenery. Jennifer was a fair-weather person in all senses of the word. She hated wet weather as much as she hated having to put herself out on another's behalf. Nobody could be more pleasant while everything was going well, but when she was crossed nobody was safe from her ire.

'It's all right,' she muttered inelegantly. 'It suits me as it is.'

His eyes mocked her. 'It certainly does!' he agreed.

Celine came suddenly to life, pointing her knife at Georgina in a manner which caused Miss Campbell to click her tongue disapprovingly. 'Georgie Porgie ran away when the others tried to play! Did you run away, Georgina?'

'Not she!' William said on a laugh. 'She gave them all a bloody nose!'

'*I did not!*' Temper flared inside Georgina. 'You and Duncan were the only two—ever!'

'The others must have been wise enough to keep their distance!' William taunted her.

To everyone's surprise and to her own consternation, her eyes brimmed with tears and they ran unchecked down her cheeks. She wiped them away with an angry hand, ashamed of displaying such weakness before her tormentor. But he was already on his feet, standing over her with his arm round her shoulders.

'Georgina, you little fraud! You've never cared before when I teased you! What did I say?'

'Nothing, nothing at all!' she sniffed dismally. 'I *like* being told how unattractive I am!'

Celine's eyes were as round as saucers. 'Georgina's crying!' she announced. 'Nobody ever cries here but me!'

'I'm sorry,' Georgina muttered.

'I think you're nice!' Celine crowed. 'You can't help being in love with William. Most married people fall in love—Stuart told me so. He says I'll fall in love one day and I won't have any more nightmares.' Her face flickered with a new anxiety. 'But I don't want to cry about it, I want to be happy! Why doesn't William make you happy?'

'He does,' Georgina claimed, her voice muffled by her hand.

'Do I?' There was a note in William's voice Georgina had never heard before. 'Then what are you crying about?'

Her face crumpled. How could she possibly tell him that? She scrubbed angrily at her cheeks and fell back on the oldest excuse in the business. 'I'm tired and I have a headache!'

He pushed the curl back from her forehead. 'Crying won't make you feel any better, my sweet. Why don't you skip the rest of dinner and go to bed?'

Georgina was very conscious of Miss Campbell's silent contempt, pointing out the inadequacies of the new mistress of the household as eloquently as if she had enumerated them one by one.

'I can't understand it!' Georgina said on a desperate note. 'I don't usually cry at all!'

Celine stabbed her knife excitedly in the air. 'You're pregnant!'

'I can't be!' Georgina wailed.

'Not yet,' William confirmed, failing to control a yelp of laughter. 'Celine, behave yourself! You're embarrassing my bride of a couple of days!'

'Is that all it is?' Georgina murmured, surprised. 'It feels much longer!'

'An old married lady!' William mocked her, but there was a new gentleness in his voice that made her heart thump so hard she felt quite faint.

'It feels like for ever!' she moaned.

The glint in his eyes was for her alone. 'It is for ever! Off you go, my sweet. Sleep tight.'

Once she was in her room, however, she didn't know what to do with herself. The sound of the rain on the roof was like distant applause and oddly soothing to her. She tried to tell herself that the rain was doing the tea a tremendous amount of good, but she didn't really care. She liked the noise it made and that was enough for her. For a few moment she sat on the edge of her bed and made herself think about William. It took all her determination and concentration not to dwell on the good bits and ignore the bad. She wanted to live again those few minutes she had spent in his arms before Celine had started screaming. Then she remembered that even then he had had Jennifer in his mind, though for once she had come out of the comparison the winner in her husband's eyes. Never had she longed more for the delicate, fair beauty of her sister than now! Just for once it would have been nice to have been Mount Everest looking down on Snowdon, instead of the other way round. Or, better still, to have been the only person in the world for William for a little while, instead of always being an also-ran, tagging along behind his greater desire for her sister.

She picked up her night things and went into the bathroom. The light spluttered and flared when she switched it on and a long peal of thunder warned of a coming storm. Hastily she switched the light off again, afraid that the whole system would blow up when she saw the stream of water that was running down the walls. There was no hot water. It was very nearly the last straw, but she calmed herself and washed as well as she could in cold water and in the dark. Thoughts of various horrid insects she had read come out from their corners in tropical rain-storms happily remained only on the fringes of her mind. What she couldn't see, she wouldn't believe in!

But she did see the gigantic shape that fleetingly went past the window. She was rooted to the spot in horror. It was taller than the house and made a peculiar rattling noise as it passed.

She flung open the window and saw it again, disappearing down the tree-lined driveway. To her relief she saw it was nothing to be afraid of after all. It was nothing more than a gigantic stuffed scarecrow with a mask instead of a head.

'Hey there!' she yelled out of the window.

The masked figure wavered to a stop and then came slowly back towards the bungalow. 'Excuse me, madam. Did you want me or something?'

'Yes. What are you doing with that thing?'

A thin, wiry man stepped from under the plaited figure. 'Excuse me, madam, someone take it away. I take it back again.'

Georgina eyed the figure with distaste. 'What is it?'

'Mahasona, madam.'

'It's hideous!'

'Oh yes, madam, but it mean nothing nowadays.' The tone was so soothing that Georgina suspected that the man wasn't half as sure about that as he pretended to be. 'We need it for the dance. This is the demon Mahasona. He gives you bad stomach, make you very ill—cholera, dysentery. Very bad demon!' He smiled with an effusiveness he obviously hoped would soften Georgina's stony expression. 'After the dance he go away and everyone keep well!'

'I hope so,' Georgina observed. 'But surely you're not going to dance now, in this rain?'

The man shook his head. 'The dance is finished, but someone took Mahasona away. Nobody mind that—but, excuse me, madam, the mask is very valuable. It is very old. It has always been used in my village. Now we don't know if the dance work.' He looked up into the skies. 'The rain brings bad stomachs, madam.'

'Will you hold the dance all over again?' Georgina asked him. If Celine were to see this plaited demon for herself, perhaps she would lose her fear of it.

'No, madam. Did madam wish to see the dance?'

Georgina nodded. 'I thought most of the dances were held down at the coast?'

'They dance too,' he agreed vaguely. He picked up the huge figure of the demon, now collapsing against the stick that formed its backbone. 'Come to the temple, madam. We make *puja*, very strong against this demon. Madam has no need to be afraid!'

Madam was not afraid. Madam was extremely angry, on the other hand. No wonder Celine had been frightened out of her wits!

'Is it heavy?' she asked suddenly. 'Could I carry it?'

The man grinned through the open window. 'Madam wishes to try?'

She climbed through the window without a second thought and struggled to hold the grips that the man pointed out to her. It was only then that she saw there were cords too that were attached to the mask and that when they were manipulated, the mask opened and shut, rolling its eyes and poking out its tongue. It was a horrible sight indeed in the almost total darkness. The whites, or yellows, showed up against the blackness of the reds and greens that only showed when they caught the light from her bedroom window. The tongue was like a snake's and, sure enough, there was a faint resemblance in the face to a bear which, coupled with the elephant-shaped head that was attached to it, was one of the most hideous sights Georgina had ever seen.

'Why, anyone could lift this,' she remarked. 'I wonder who did?'

'Very bad thing, madam.'

'Very!' she retorted with feeling. 'I'd like to see it again in the light of day. Would your village mind?'

'No, Madam. Mr Kotalawala will bring you to the village if you ask him. I will tell the priest you are coming.'

'Thank you. I'll be bringing another girl with me. Will that matter?'

'Madam Celine.' He grinned, rolling his eyes. 'Madam Celine is always welcome among us. The little madam too!'

Georgina found herself laughing with him. 'My name is Georgina. I'm married to William Ayres.'

'The man who makes the river flow backwards? A good man!'

'Yes,' said Georgina, and was surprised to find she meant it, 'he is a very good man—and a generous one too. I'm sure he'll be properly grateful if we can reassure Celine that what she saw was this and not some figment of her imagination. Only who can have wanted to scare her with such a silly trick?'

The man looked puzzled. 'My name is Rabahindre, madam.'

Georgina shook him warmly by the hand. 'I'll be seeing you, Mr Rabahindre,' she said.

The man laughed and wagged his head. 'Not Mister—Rabahindre only. Madam and I are friends, no?'

Georgina smiled back at him. 'I hope so,' she said.

It was much more difficult getting back through the

window. She made one or two abortive attempts and then gave up the struggle and went round to the front door, hoping she would find it open. It was not. Feeling rather foolish, she banged on the solid wood portals, now wet through from the rain. The door swung open and William stood in the floodlit doorway, staring at her in open astonishment.

'How did you get out?' he demanded.

'Through the bathroom window.' She slipped past him into the hall, dripping water on to the floor. 'I saw Celine's demon. He's the demon of cholera and dysentery and his head has to be the most hideous thing I've ever seen. Rabahindre says we can go and look at it in daylight if we want to. He said someone took it away from his village and brought it up here. He wasn't best pleased about it.'

'And you went out like that?'

Georgina looked down at herself, noting the way the wet cloth of her thin dress clung to the shape of her body. 'He'd have gone if I'd waited to get a coat,' she said defensively. 'Besides, it's dark outside.'

'Well, it isn't dark in here,' said William. He put his hands on her shoulders, turned her round until she had her back to him and forcibly propelled her down the wide corridor to her bedroom door.

'Aren't you pleased?' Georgina shot at him over her shoulder. His hands felt warm and intimate and hard and masculine against her shoulders.

'That you're doing your best to drown yourself when you ought to be tucked up in your bed?'

'No, silly, that Celine *did* see her demon!'

His hands dropped to her waist. 'Damn all demons! For heaven's sake, go to bed, Georgina, and this time stay there! Can you manage, or shall I send Miss Campbell to you?'

She leaned back against him, weakened by his touch. 'I can manage. I don't require Miss Campbell's services ever!

William, are you coming to bed too?'

His hands squeezed her so tightly she cried out. 'Not tonight, Josephine,' he said, turning on his heel. 'Tonight you look like a cross between a drowned rat and my canary——'

'Charming!'

'More charming than you know!' he flung over his shoulder. 'All the curves in the right places and our marriage lines in my pocket.'

The tip of her tongue protruded against her upper lip. 'Well then?'

'Go to bed, Georgina. By yourself!'

Her eyes fell before the look in his. 'Because I'm not Jennifer? I'll never be she, though! Can't you——'

'Not tonight, Georgina!'

'Then I'd rather you didn't come calling at all!' she shot at him mutinously. 'I don't like you any better now than I did when you were fifteen! You were horrid as a boy, and you're equally horrid now!'

He was graceless enough to laugh at her. 'I haven't got a scarlet racing-cycle now. Is there some new attraction?'

She was down the corridor towards him before she had thought, intent only on wiping the smile off his face, but this time he was ready for her. He caught her up between arms of steel and carried her into her room, dropping her from a height on to the centre of her bed.

'Be thankful you look enough like Little Girl Lost in the storm for me not to turn you over my knee, Georgie Porgie!' He bent down and kissed her hard on the mouth. 'Goodnight, Georgina!'

Her lips felt stiff and the warm masculinity of his lingered long after he had gone. 'Goodnight, William,' she said to the empty room, and her voice sounded as weak and vulnerable as she felt. And still the rain came down, pounding a tattoo on the tin roof of the bathroom. Georgina lay there and listened to it for a long, long time before she struggled off the bed and changed out of her wet clothes into her nightdress and, pulling the sheet up over her head, went fast asleep.

Stuart Duffield stretched his legs out in front of him and allowed Celine to press some lemons into a glass and add iced water and sugar for him. He watched her every movement, Georgina noticed, an oddly contented expression on his face.

'So you girls want me to escort you down to the village?' he said. 'How did you get to hear about their dances? I shouldn't have thought either of you were the type to be interested in demonology.'

'Not as such,' Georgina affirmed. 'Just one demon, Mahasona, whose image apparently walked out of the village and all the way up to the bungalow by itself. It scared Celine silly, and I'm not at all surprised. It has the most hideous face I've ever seen.'

Stuart's interest was caught. 'You saw it too?'

'I saw it being taken back to the village by one Rabahindre. I want to see it again in daylight when it will be a lot less scary. I'd like to know who played such a silly trick on us too, but I'm not hopeful about that.'

'What did Rabahindre say?'

'Nothing. But he did invite us all to a ceremony at the Hindu temple. I don't think he knows how it got here any more than we do. His chief concern was the mask the creature wore. Apparently it's old and valuable. It's certainly hideous!'

Celine's hand shook, clinking the ice in her glass. 'I didn't see a mask, Georgina. I keep telling you, it moved! It drank some red stuff that looked like blood out of an elephant's head. A mask couldn't do that!'

'We'll see,' said Georgina. 'I'm almost sure this one could.'

Celine looked unhappy. 'But I'm always seeing things

like that. It's nothing new. I'm touched in the head—I have been ever since my mother died in that fire. My father took me from hospital to hospital to find out what was the matter with me, but none of them ever found out. Mostly they thought it was caused by guilt because I wasn't sorry when my mother died.'

The look of shock on Stuart's face was enough to tell Georgina that this was far more than Celine had ever said on the subject before. What was more, she had said it in the lucid terms an adult would use to describe her case, not at all as the child she usually pretended to be.

'I never believe in figments of the imagination until there's absolutely no other possible solution,' Georgina answered in matter-of-fact tones. 'Your other demons probably have a similar explanation if anyone had cared to look for it.'

'But I wasn't sorry when Mother died,' Celine told her.

'I don't suppose you felt anything. One doesn't when one's shocked. Everyone knows that, Celine!'

'Father thought I was mad. He didn't like being with me afterwards. He was never at home, though Miss Campbell was always telling him I would be better if I saw a little more of him. She was in love with him.'

Stuart hooted with laughter. 'Miss Campbell?' he snorted.

Celine opened her eyes very wide. 'The ugly have to make up in other ways,' she explained carefully. 'She wanted him for herself long before Mother died. I felt sorry for her. Mother didn't lift a finger where Father was concerned—she was always out with other men and things like that. It didn't seem fair. You wouldn't understand, Georgina, because men like you, but if they don't, what does one do then?'

Georgina was shocked into spilling her drink. 'Darling, anyone as beautiful as you are——'

'Has to look out!' Celine finished for her. 'I've known

that for a long time. Beauty inspires hatred, not love. That's why Miss Campbell hates me. She was jealous of my mother, but she can't be jealous of me, can she? I'm not likely to take any man away from her.'

Georgina stared at her. 'Does she hate you?'

Celine nodded. 'She only stayed to be close to Father.'

'Then why stay now?' Georgina prompted her.

But Celine's glance wandered away from hers, whether deliberately or not it was impossible to say. 'William says she's going away!' she remarked in delight. 'I hope she does go, but she never has gone in the past. Sometimes I think she'll stay with me for ever and ever!'

Georgina made to speak, but Stuart stopped her, putting his hand over hers, his fingers tightening to gain her attention.

'Celine, why do you stay with her?' he asked.

She smiled a wry smile. 'How unobservant you are! Because I'm only ten pence in the shilling, or whatever the expression is. I'm afraid of being on my own. I see things that scare me, and I have frightful nightmares and, when that happens, even someone one hates is better than nobody at all!'

'You ought to get married,' he suggested.

Her mouth trembled and she shrugged her shoulders. 'Nobody'd have me!' she said.

It was Georgina who was first aware that William had come out on to the verandah to join them. She hadn't seen him since the night before and the colour rose like a tide in her cheeks as she realised he had seen the way Stuart had his hand over hers. She snatched her own away, looking inexplicably guilty.

'The sun's shining,' she said foolishly. 'It all looks different in the sun, doesn't it?'

William tossed a letter down on to her lap. 'Does it look more or less romantic?' he challenged her.

She had no answer, so she busied herself opening her

letter, delighted to have one so soon from her family. 'Goodness!' she exclaimed as she read the opening paragraph. 'Jennifer wants to get away from Duncan's reproaches. She wants to come and visit us here. She's hopeful!'

William took the letter from her and began to read it aloud: 'Poor Jennie misses you unbearably, my dear, as she always did when you were away. She has so few friends of her own and yours seldom come when you're not here to receive them. I wonder why? Your father and I have always thought she has by far the nicer nature. Perhaps we were wrong to insist she always looked up to you as the elder sister. Poor poppet, she was dreadfully upset over your marriage to William and she never let anyone guess it at the time. I must say, Georgie, I think you very wrong to have come between them. I know she thought she wanted Duncan, but you might have known that would never come to anything. None of us can understand why you let her talk you into telling William in the first place, unless of course you wanted him for yourself? One can't help feeling sorry for him when you think what he might have had!'

'It's from my mother,' Georgina said unnecessarily. She snatched the letter back from him. 'And it's addressed to me! If I want to tell you what's in it, I will when I've finished it. You may be my husband, but you have no right to read my letters in my book!'

William's eyes narrowed. 'Is Jennifer your father's favourite too?' he asked her.

Hurt to the quick, she refused to meet his eyes, but buried herself in her letter instead, mumbling something about her father not playing favourites. 'One can't help liking one person more than another, though,' she added. 'You should know that!'

He relaxed, throwing himself into the nearest canvas chair. 'I do,' he admitted. 'Are you going to let Jennifer come?'

Georgina hunched her shoulders. 'Have I any choice?'

Stuart finished his drink and rose quickly to his feet. 'I'm off,' he announced. 'Thanks for the drink. I'll call for you around tea time, girls. Will that do?'

He smiled at Georgina, ruffled Celine's hair with a friendly hand, and was gone, leaving a silence one could cut with a knife behind him.

'What attraction is bringing him back this afternoon?' William enquired, his gaze noting with interest the fluctuating colour in his wife's face. 'You?'

'He's taking us to the village,' Celine answered him. 'To see if the demon Georgina saw last night is the same one that I saw.'

William raised a thoughtful brow. 'Good. I think I'll come too and keep an eye on this wife of mine.'

'You don't have to,' Georgina protested.

'Don't I? What I have, I hold, Georgina Ayres. You won't cuckold me lightly, not even with such an easy-going partner as Stuart Duffield——'

Georgina raised wide, astonished eyes. 'But——'

'I should have accepted your invitation last night, shouldn't I, my sweet? I didn't awaken you to love to have someone else steal the cream! Stuart will have to look else-where——'

'What about Jennifer?' Georgina cut him off, hotly embarrassed.

'What about her?' he retorted. '*She* isn't my wife!'

'But how you wish she were! Do you want her to come, or not?'

'Invite her by all means,' he answered smoothly. 'It won't make any difference to us, I assure you. Much as I hate to ruffle your romantic dreams, my dear, her coming won't alter the fact that *you* are mine. Hanker after Stuart all you please, you're staying mine! He and Jennifer will be the ones who'll play games together——'

'Then I don't want her here!' Celine burst into the argument. 'Stuart is *my* friend. I don't like the sound of this silly Jennifer! Why can't she stay in England?'

Georgina could only wonder the same, but she knew her sister well enough to know that nothing she could say or do would make her stay away if she had made up her mind to come.

'I'll write to her,' she said dully. 'With any luck she won't come!'

But that was too much to hope for, just as William may have said that she was his, but would never, never admit that he was in any way hers. If he did, just once, a hundred Jennifers could come to Sri Lanka and be welcome!

# CHAPTER EIGHT

Georgina was glad to be quiet for a few moments. She had never had an easy chair in her bedroom before, but these last few minutes had convinced her that it was a very good idea. Nobody would disturb her in her own room and she needed some time by herself to calm down and do a bit of hard thinking about what she was going to do about Jennifer. When she thought of her mother's letter she still burned with embarrassment, and that William should have read it was the last straw! He would think all the worse of her now that he knew that even her parents thought more highly of Jennifer than they did of herself.

There was Celine to be considered too. Georgina had been on the receiving end of Jennifer's sharp tongue too often not to know how she would make the younger girl suffer for having the kind of beauty that Jennifer had always been led to believe she possessed herself. Only when the sun shone, as Shakespeare had pointed out, the light of a candle paled into insignificance. Jennifer would not like Celine at all!

Then there was William. He might be possessive, but he was far from loving as far as Georgina was concerned. Jennifer was a different cup of tea. Jennifer was the love of his life and only Georgina would stand between them and the consummation of that love. And she was not such a fool as not to know that Jennifer would give him every encouragement. The mere fact that William was her husband would be enough to force her sister to go to any lengths to get him away from her. One way and another, it wasn't a very pleasant prospect actually to have her in the same house, the first home she had ever tried to share with William.

Outside the window was a frangipani tree, or temple tree as it was more often called locally. Georgina watched the white flowers dance in the light breeze and thought how different today was from yesterday. The sun was shining, for one thing, drawing some of the moisture out of the fertile ground in little puffs of steam. Otherwise the rain of yesterday might never have been. When she stood up, she could see a sloping garden, very English in character, that led down to a hollow where a table and chairs were permanently laid out, taking it for granted that most meals would be taken out of doors. Was that where they would have lunch? she wondered.

'Georgie, are you in there?'

If she kept very quiet perhaps he would go away. She had not yet forgiven William for reading her mother's letter. Besides, she felt too raw to embark on another skirmish with him before lunch. She would say something she would regret, something that would confirm him in his belief she was jealous of her sister, when she truly didn't think she was, not while she was thousands of miles away and there was no possibility of her benefiting from William's decided partiality for her rather than for his own wife.

The door opened and William walked in, taking in her small figure seated on the rather large chair in a single glance.

'What are you doing?' he asked her. 'Sulking?'

She shook her head. 'I was wondering what to do about Jennifer.'

He gave her a long, hard look. 'Wouldn't it be more to the point to wonder where you're going with your husband?'

Her eyes fell before his. 'You had no right to read my mother's letter without my permission,' she said stiffly.

'How would you like it if I were to read your letters?'

He shrugged. 'You can read them any time you choose. You do anyway.'

'I do not!'

'No? Do you still claim you didn't read Jennifer's letter to me, or hold it up until it was too late for me to do anything about it?'

'Yes, I do. Anyone would think it was I who forced you to the altar instead of the other way round!'

'Oh, not that again! Really, Georgie, nobody could have made you marry me if you hadn't allowed them to.'

'I wish I hadn't!'

His expression took on a grimness she had not seen before. 'So I noticed. Somehow I'd never thought of you as being particularly susceptible to the blandishments of my sex. Jennifer yes, but not you.'

She looked up at him then, giving him a roguish look because, at that moment, it was the best defence she had. 'Why not me?' she asked.

'Maybe you had no opportunity before to bask in the admiration of your male acquaintances because Jennifer was always in your way, but things are different now. I don't know how it is, but there's something different about you since we came to Sri Lanka. You're inviting trouble, do you know that? I'm not surprised young Stuart can hardly keep his hands off you!'

Georgina summoned up a laugh. 'Don't be ridiculous! He can't take his eyes off Celine—and a very good thing too! She's much more normal when he's around, and she likes him very much. That's what bothers me about Jennifer coming here. It wouldn't occur to her to notice how Celine feels about Stuart. She'd dismiss her as a child and her feelings as being of no account to anyone! Jennifer never sees anyone's point of view but her own.'

'Meaning she's never worried much about yours?' he ground out.

'I never minded before!' she answered.

'Never?' His disbelief was total. 'What about her engagement to me?'

Had she minded? Honesty forced Georgina to admit to herself that she had, though at the time she would have laughed any such idea to scorn, but she would not admit as much to William.

'It was a way of getting back at you when it was all over. As far I was concerned that was all there was to it!'

'You took Jennifer's place——'

'I didn't think I had any choice!'

He put a hand on either arm of her chair. 'You didn't. I meant to have you, and have you I will, my Georgie Porgie! What's more, I'll break your pretty neck for you if I see you playing patsy with Stuart again!'

His closeness made her heart pound. She tried to breathe normally, but somehow she couldn't get any air into her lungs.

'You wouldn't dare say such a thing to Jennifer!' she challenged him in a small voice.

'You underrate me! No woman will ever rule me, Georgina, however much they might like to. Not Jennifer, and not you!'

She had never lacked courage, but it was put to the test then as she stared back, deep into his golden eyes. 'You take too much on yourself, William Ayres. If you think I'm going to sit down under such a Victorian attitude, while you read my letters and vet my friends, you're very much mistaken! I'll make my own decisions!'

'Will you, my Georgie?' His face softened into amusement and she hated him for it, for it was the amusement of the victor when he knows that nothing is going to stop him from getting his own way. 'Women are at a biological disadvantage when it comes to some decisions. Diana the Huntress remained a virgin goddess, if you remember——'

'Perhaps I may choose to do so too!'

'You can try!' he mocked her. 'But I'd hedge my bets if I were you. You may have got away with it at one time, little one, but that was before I had your measure. Are you afraid I'm not going to be man enough for you?'

She couldn't have answered to save her life. 'Well?' he prompted her.

She swallowed, averting her eyes from his. 'This is an impossible conversation!' she declared. 'Why should you want to make my decisions for me anyway?'

He bent his elbows, bringing his face very close to hers. 'Because you prefer it that way, little fraud. You'd run even now, if I let you, wouldn't you? Cutting off your nose to spite your face? What a girl! I won't fancy your kisses any more if you spread them around the neighbourhood in a series of trial runs. I'll teach my own wife all she needs to know, and I won't hesitate to call her to heel if she strays too far away from me——'

'I see!' she cut him off. 'It's a matter of pride and I'm cast in the role of propping up your ego! What if I won't do it?'

His lips parted in a smile. They were so close to her that she could feel his breath on her own. 'Care to try it?' he murmured on a note of laughter.

Her heart turned over within her. 'No,' she whispered.

'I thought not.' His lips touched hers and drew back again. '*Sugar and spice and all things nice, that's what little girls are made of*, Georgie Porgie. Don't spoil it by over-doing the spice. It's the sugar that turns me on!'

She put up a hand and touched his cheek. 'That's all it means to you, isn't it? A turn on?'

His lips took a long, slow toll of hers. 'I'll let you know,' he murmured. 'Damn it all, Georgie, you are my wife!'

'Big deal!' Her other arm slipped up round the back of his neck. 'How much will that mean to you when Jennifer gets here?'

He released himself with the greatest of ease. 'That

depends on you,' he answered, walking over to the window and standing there with his back to her. 'You have the advantage if you care to use it, but do you?'

'What advantage?'

He cast her a mocking glance. 'If you play your cards right Jennifer could be just a memory by the time she gets here. Until I have to report on site for my work, I'm all yours!'

'Oh yes?' Her tone was every bit as dry as his. 'Don't you mean that I'm all yours? Or at least, isn't that what you'd like to mean?'

'I mean we're stuck with one another,' he answered, and quoted softly: *'As unto the bow the cord is, So unto the man is woman; Though she bends him, she obeys him, Though she draws him, yet she follows; Useless each without the other.'*

'Only if they're tied to one another,' she objected.

'And aren't we tied by marriage?'

She sniffed. 'I might have known you'd like Victorian poets as much as you do their ideas of male superiority. Nobody quotes *Hiawatha* nowadays!' She took a deep breath. 'You're not stuck with me, William, unless you want to be. I'd never hold you to such an unprofitable arrangement. I want to be the only woman in the world for my husband, not a piece of tatty string!'

He turned and faced her. 'Poor Georgie! Ever the romantic under that practical exterior of yours! It's an intriguing combination. Dream your dreams, my dear, and who knows, they may come true for you. Perhaps you approve of Nietzsche more than you do of Longfellow? *Only he who is man enough will release the woman in woman,* and Stuart and his kind will never be man enough for you!'

'But you are?'

He was openly amused. 'At the risk of your thinking me even more conceited than you do now, yes, I am.'

'You can't know that!'

He put his hands on his hips and laughed at her, a great bellow of sound that rang round the silent bungalow.

'For heaven's sake!' she rebuked him. 'What did you have to do that for? Miss Campbell will wonder what on earth we're doing!'

That made him laugh again. 'Do you care?' he asked, his eyes dancing.

'Yes, I do,' Georgina answered him soberly. 'I think Miss Campbell a dangerous woman and I wouldn't want to stir her into any further activity like the demon of last night.'

'Miss Campbell?'

She nodded. 'Who else, William? Who else would want to frighten Celine into a scene?'

'I don't know, my dear, but do you think Miss Campbell has the imagination to make use of such a thing? She and Celine haven't been here long, only a few days before we arrived ourselves, and she's not the type to go down to the village by herself. It was probably just a coincidence.'

Georgina had her own doubts, but she was not prepared to give voice to them. 'She looks like a witch,' she said instead. 'Perhaps she is one.'

William gave her a startled look. 'If she is one she'd have had a job to persuade the Aborigines to allow her to make use of their sacred objects. It was the sound of a whirring rope that set Celine off in Australia. It always began the same way—and ended in her being frightened into a fit. One of the Australian doctors we consulted suggested she might have witnessed some Aboriginal ceremony as a child, some thing she wasn't supposed to see, and that it had haunted her ever since.'

'That's no excuse for Miss Campbell telling her she's touched in the head!' Georgina said sharply. 'That was cruel!'

William studied her face with a thoughtful look. 'Women don't always examine their weapons with sufficient care before they throw them, Georgina. You should know that!'

'I've never tried to drive anyone mad!'

They stared at one another in mutual consternation, but Georgina couldn't bring herself to take the words back.

'But why?' William asked.

Georgina laced her fingers together. 'I don't know. Celine says she was in love with her father. William, that woman has to go!'

'She'll expect to serve out her notice and I have no reasonable excuse for sending her away before the month is out. I agree she has to go, but don't overrate Celine's lucidity, will you? She'll never be more than a little girl at heart—that was about the only thing the doctors were agreed about! There's no point in encouraging her to start thinking of love and romance when she can never be a wife.'

'I don't see why she can't be. She's a lovely girl.'

William's lips twisted into a wry smile. 'A man wants more than mere beauty in his wife,' he said.

But *he* didn't! He wanted Jennifer, and what for, if not for her delicate beauty? The answer to that hurt so badly that Georgina felt it like a physical pain inside her. When one loved, beauty didn't matter, *nothing* mattered except the joy one felt in the beloved's presence. That was how she felt about William. That was what was so awful about it, that he didn't feel the same way about her and he never would.

'Celine has a lot more than beauty to recommend her,' she said aloud. 'I'm sure Stuart sees her as something more than a little girl. I know I do.'

'Despite the scene last night?'

Georgina nodded. 'That was fright. We're none of us ourselves when we're badly frightened. At other times Celine is as lucid as you or I. That blank look she puts on is probably a defence she's grown up with. Anyone would if they had to put up with Miss Campbell all day and every day.'

William grinned. 'So you don't like Miss Campbell, Georgie Porgie, but I couldn't have managed without her— nor could Celine's father! How d'you suppose he would have looked after Celine on his own? He had his work to do. He couldn't have had a retarded daughter hanging on to his sleeve all the time.'

Georgina looked down at her hands, trying to stop herself from entering into an argument on such slight evidence that even she could see she had formed her opinion largely on guesswork and a hunch that, despite its implications, wouldn't go away.

'And what were Miss Campbell's rewards?' she asked.

William froze. 'What do you mean?'

'Only that her major interest doesn't seem to be money, does it?'

William hauled her up on to her feet and into his arms. She hid her face against him, trying to still the trembling that had seized her limbs. He smelt nice, she decided, but then she liked everything about him. His attraction for her was so strong she felt quite dizzy with it. His fingers found the nape of her neck and closed about it, before entangling themselves in her hair and forcing her face up to meet his.

'Why is it never the right time for me to kiss you properly?' he demanded in her ear. 'I can't and won't wait for ever, Georgie Porgie!'

She shuddered against him, saying nothing. There was a lump in her throat the size of a tennis ball and she swallowed helplessly, trying to make it go away. It didn't. On the contrary, it grew so large she was afraid it would dissolve into a flood of tears and he would think it was something he had done to her.

'Don't you want me to kiss you?' he asked, smoothing the curl away from her forehead. 'Don't you think you could try to kiss me too?'

'I——' She swallowed again as he bent his head bringing his lips within half an inch of her own. 'I can't!' she blurted out.

'Why not?' he murmured, touching his mouth to hers. 'You like that well enough, my Georgie!'

She liked it far too much! 'It's lunchtime——'

'I'd rather have you for lunch!'

'No! Oh no!' She stepped back from him in a panic and found herself still held by her hair. 'William, we can't! Not now!'

His lips twitched in ready amusement. 'I won't let you go until you kiss me, Georgie Porgie.' He wiped away a tear from her eye with a gentle finger. 'And this time there'll be no tears from either of us, huh?'

She wriggled desperately, found she couldn't get free from him that way, and tried kicking his shins instead. It was a mistake. His fingers tightened in her hair and his other arm lifted her clear off the ground, placing her firmly on his knee as he collapsed into the chair she had only recently vacated.

'Still determined to be the little thug we all know and love?' he taunted her. 'You ought to know by now it won't work with me, my Georgie! Now kiss me properly, my love, or take the consequences!'

'I won't!' She glared at him, her heart beating so fast she thought she might faint and that she might even welcome such an escape at that moment.

'You will if you want any lunch, my pet.' A smile flickered across his face and the unwelcome suspicion crossed her mind that he was enjoying himself. 'How will you explain your non-appearance at the village?' he added in the same, conversational tones. 'Young Stuart will be disappointed.'

'He's not all that much younger than you are!' she declared.

'You think not?' He turned the matter over in his mind.

'He's young enough to let you make the running, but you're too feminine to put up with that for long! Aren't you, Georgie?'

'I prefer it to being patronised!' she shot back at him.

'Ah, but you are mine to treat with as I please,' he teased her, his eyes alight with laughter as he waited for the coming explosion.

'Then you can't complain if I treat you just as I like!'

'You can try!' He lifted an eyebrow in derision. 'You should listen more closely, sweetheart. I did say "treat with", but I daresay one way is as good as the other with you.'

'I won't be browbeaten——'

'My dear little Georgie, what's much more to the point is neither will I! Come, kiss me of your own free will and we'll cry a truce for the afternoon, if that will please my lady?'

She brooded over his words, knowing herself to be caught in a cleft stick. Nor was she as reluctant as she pretended. She leaned away from him, gazing at him thoughtfully, liking her position far better than she would have him know.

'And if I do kiss you? Will you be content with that?'

'For now,' he drawled. He looked sleepy and not at all dangerous. 'One good kiss on the lips, Georgina!'

Her eyes widened as her one line of retreat was cut off. She spread her hand across the opening of his shirt, giving herself a little more time to make up her mind what to do next. The hairs on his chest created a *frisson* of pleasure against her fingers.

'You're easily pleased if that's all you want,' she said at last. 'Wouldn't you rather wait until I offer to kiss you without being forced?'

He shut his eyes entirely. 'When will that be?'

A cautious reconnoitre informed her that he was confident enough to have relinquished his hold over her. She patted his cheek gently, delighted with her own cleverness, and made to get off his knee, only to find herself caught more firmly than before.

'Cheat!' he said mildly. His eyes opened and they were full of a lazy amusement that brought the colour to her face and a singing to her ears. 'Give in, Georgina,' he recommended her. 'You're not going to get your own way this time no matter how you twist and turn.' He smiled at her outraged expression. 'What's a little kiss between friends?'

'We're not friends!'

He gave her a quizzical look, but he said nothing, waiting for her to make the next move. And she would have to, she thought, for he plainly meant to go on sitting there until she did.

'I think you're mean!' she informed him roundly. 'Why should you want me to kiss you?'

'I wonder!' he mocked her.

She tried another tack. 'I think you should woo me a little first,' she said.

'My dear girl, what else have I been doing ever since we arrived in Sri Lanka!'

Had he——? Was it possible——? His laughter demoralised her completely and she thumped him on the chest.

'Oh, *you*!' she exclaimed. But she was half glad he had defeated her. Her body tensed as she put her mouth to his and she kissed him as a child might kiss an adult under protest. 'There!'

'That was a kiss? You have a lot to learn, Georgie! Come back where you were and I'll show you what I mean by a kiss!'

She relaxed into a delicious surrender that only wanted to please him and thereby herself. She felt his hands on her back and on the soft curve of her breast and dug her own fingers into the hair of his chest.

'That's better!' William murmured. His voice sounded

husky but the mockery was still very much in evidence. 'Who said you couldn't kiss if you tried?'

'But it wasn't me kissing you!' she crowed in triumph.

'No?' The flecks of gold in his eyes reminded her of fireworks. 'Then what were you doing?'

She decided it was a rhetorical question undeserving of an answer. 'May I go now?' she countered on her own behalf.

He raised his hands, freeing her from his embrace. 'If you want to.'

It wasn't fair, but then he never did play fair. She could only hope that he didn't know how little she wanted to drag herself off his knee. She went over to the dressing table and seated herself in front of the looking-glass, running a comb through her hair without bothering to see what she was doing. There was no reason why she shouldn't kiss her own husband, she comforted herself, annoyed by the guilty excitement that had reduced her to an eager participant in the embrace. What was there in a kiss to make her want more and more of the same?

William came up behind her and took the comb from her hand, finishing off the job for her, a half-smile curving his lips as he did so. His eyes looked her over with appreciation in the glass.

'Did you mind so much?' he asked her, when he had finished and was putting the comb down on the table in front of her.

She made a gesture to avoid answering, but as her eyes met his in the glass, she knew she was being less than generous. She turned away, fingering the ring on her finger with a nervous touch.

'No,' she said at last and, jumping to her feet, she practically ran out of the room.

Celine was waiting for her on the verandah. She looked up anxiously as Georgina hurtled through the french window, her cheeks flaming with a very becoming colour.

'Georgina, may I speak to you now?' she begged. 'You do like me a little bit, don't you? I mean, you don't like anyone here better than me, do you?'

Only William. 'No,' Georgina agreed vaguely.

'That's good! I was afraid you liked Stuart.' Celine frowned. 'William thinks you do.'

'I like him well enough,' Georgina admitted. 'I hardly know him.'

'Oh dear,' said Celine, 'I was afraid of that. I think—I think he likes you too.'

Georgina gave her an impatient look. 'What are you talking about?' she demanded.

Celine's face crumpled. 'I thought you'd understand!' she wailed. 'But you're just like all the rest of them. You don't think I can feel anything, but I do!'

'Oh, Celine, I'm so sorry,' Georgina said at once. 'I wasn't really listening. I was thinking about—something else. I didn't mean to be nasty, or to snub you or anything.'

Celine smiled, the sunshine breaking through the threatened shower of rain. 'I was talking about Stuart. Georgina, have you ever been in love?'

Georgina was on the point of saying no, but something in the other girl's face prevented her. 'Why?' she asked instead.

'Well, you can't be in love with William. He'd know if you were because he's married to you. And *he* thinks you and Stuart might fall in love with each other. He said so! Only I couldn't bear it if you did!'

Georgina's look was scandalised. 'How many men do you think I want?' But Celine was unamused. 'Oh, Celine, really! William was talking about something else. He knows as well as you do that I'm not going to fall in love with Stuart! And as for him, I hardly think my looks would appeal much when he has only to turn his head and look at you. You're the one who's beautiful, my pet, not me!'

'But you have something else——'

'*Me?*' Georgina laughed at the very idea. 'You should ask my sister about that! She's the one who has the looks in our family and attracts all the attention, though even she would pale into insignificance beside you! I think you're the loveliest person I've ever seen.'

Celine looked merely uncomfortable. 'It's nice of you to say so, Georgie, but I don't think you know much about things like that after all.' She looked up appealingly. 'You're welcome to William, but not to Stuart as well! I wasn't going to tell you—I wasn't going to tell anyone because they'll only laugh at me, but I love Stuart and I want him to love me.'

'If you ask me, he hasn't far to go! Why don't you tell him how you feel, Celine?'

'If it's true and your demon is the one I saw, I'll think about it. I won't otherwise. Stuart deserves the very best, not a retarded idiot——'

Georgina put on a severe expression. 'I won't have you speak of yourself like that!' she cut in. 'Don't ever say such a thing again, Celine!'

'Don't you believe it?' the other girl asked.

'No, I don't! And Stuart won't either!'

'Then you don't mind, Georgie? I know you only have to lift your little finger——' She bit her lip. 'I expect it's always been the same for you!'

Coming on to the verandah, William caught Celine's last plea. He put his arm round the girl's shoulders, smiling down at her.

'Surely you're not afraid of competition from Georgie?' he teased her. 'Jennifer never had any trouble from her.'

'Then Georgie wasn't trying! I don't like the sound of Jennifer anyway. She sounds silly and spoilt, and Georgie isn't either of those things. I'll bet most people prefer her really!'

'Do you?' William appeared to have lost interest. 'I shouldn't put my shirt on it, if I were you.'

Celine flounced away from him indignantly. 'You're a fool, William!' she told him over her shoulder. '*You* preferred her, didn't you? And so would Stuart if she wanted him!'

William favoured her with a lazy smile. 'What makes you think I prefer her?' he asked.

Celine looked him straight in the eye, ignoring Georgina's ineffectual protest. 'Because you married her,' she said with considerable violence, 'and because you're glad you did! You've been glad ever since!' The blank look came over her face like the ringing down of a curtain. 'Shall we go in to lunch?' she said.

# CHAPTER NINE

Georgina had never stood back and compared William to any other man before, but she did so now, watching him and Stuart as they stood side by side, making desultory conversation while they waited for Celine and her to join them. To an objective observer, the slighter man had to be considered the more handsome, but she was far from being able to make such an objective judgment. It was William who tugged at her heartstrings and whose smile reduced her knees to jelly. Besides, she liked his largeness, both in mind and body. Indeed, she couldn't think of anything she didn't like about him! Bad luck to her, she thought, if she couldn't keep her emotions under better control. Under the very best of circumstances William would be a hard man to hold, and her circumstances could hardly be worse.

Stuart had brought his jeep and they all piled in, the women sitting in the back to allow the men more leg room.

'Are you all right back there?' William asked, smiling an ironical smile at his wife.

'Would it matter if we were not?' she returned.

'You could always sit on my knee!'

She blushed. 'And what about Celine?'

'I hardly think there would be room for both of you.'

'Then I'll stay where I am!'

Having got that settled, Stuart drove off through the close by tea gardens, some of them planted on such steep hills that Georgina wondered that the Tamil women could balance themselves to pick the precious leaves. In their brightly coloured saris they looked as pretty as butterflies, making their way up and down the long lines of bushes, picking with both hands as they went. They wore some specialy made baskets on their backs which they filled up at lightning speed, untiring in their urgency to earn the extra bonuses that were paid to anyone who picked more than the minimum weight required.

'Do they all come from South India?' she asked Stuart.

'Originally, I daresay a high proportion of these were born here in Ceylon, but they still think of their home as being in India. It's hard to believe, but many of their relatives back home in the mother country are even poorer than the Tamils here. Many of them send a large proportion of their earnings back to India. That's part of the trouble, because Sri Lanka can't afford the drain on her resources and the Tamils get caught between the pressures on both sides of the argument. Someone will have to think of an answer soon, though. Many of them are worse than poor—the whole island is poor!—but some of the Tamils are actually starving.'

'Why did they come?' Georgina asked.

Stuart made a wry face. 'We, the British, imported them to work the tea estates. They're much more amenable to long hours of repetitive, dull work than are the Sinhalese—especially the women. There's no doubt they've been let down somewhere along the line. Tea is very important to the Lankan economy and they ought to benefit accordingly. But when one tries to apportion the blame it becomes much more difficult. All kinds of political platforms are mounted by all kinds of people and they all make a great deal of noise. Meanwhile the Tamils fall further and further behind in the subsistence stakes.'

'Can't we do something?'

Stuart pooh-poohed the idea. 'Our hands are hardly clean enough for anyone to want to listen! Until recently many of these estates were British owned and nothing was done then for them. It would be a case of the pot calling the kettle black with a vengeance!'

Georgina sighed. 'But on this estate——'

'Things are pretty good here,' Stuart agreed. 'The best tea is grown high up, and one can hardly get higher than here. We get the best prices and offer our workers the best conditions accordingly. Some of our tea is so highly thought of that if one were to buy it in London it would cost all of seven pounds a pound. Nobody will pay that, so it gets mixed in with other grades. When I take you over the factory you'll be able to try your hand at my job and find out how good your taste-buds are. I never drink alcohol or eat spicy food in case I lose my touch, but it has other rewards. Tea is a fascinating crop.'

Celine leaned forward eagerly to catch the full import of his words. Her eyes were bright and alive with interest. It was a far cry from the apathetic, lacklustre child she sometimes appeared to be.

'I didn't want to leave Australia, but I'm awfully glad now that William made me come. He doesn't usually want Miss Campbell and me around when he's working and we just stick at home. But I wouldn't have missed all this for anything!'

'Miss Campbell might have been happier back home,' William said dryly.

'Who cares? I love it here! She's cross because you only gave her a few hours to pack up all our things. She didn't want to come.'

Georgina laughed. 'I'm glad she hasn't succeeded in putting you off Sri Lanka,' she said. 'It wouldn't be the same here without you.'

Celine blinked with pleasurable disbelief. 'I didn't want to come because *she* didn't,' she blurted out. 'She doesn't like it when William comes the heavy guardian, you see. She likes to be the only one to tell me what to do.'

Georgina put a comforting hand on the girl's shoulder. 'If William comes the heavy guardian too often you should send him about his business,' she advised. 'You're old enough to make your own decisions. Don't you agree, Stuart?'

Stuart cast a quick look at the lovely, fair girl, giving nothing away. 'I like her the way she is,' he said.

Celin giggled nervously. 'And how am I?'

'Gentle and biddable,' he replied promptly. 'I can't abide pushy women!'

'Like Georgina,' William put in at once.

'*Georgina?*' Stuart exclaimed, almost running the jeep off the road. 'There's nothing wrong with Georgie.'

Georgina cast her husband a look of malicious triumph. 'Thank you, Stuart,' she murmured meekly. 'It's nice to be appreciated for a change.'

William uttered a snort of laughter. 'Oh, I appreciate you all right, Georgie Porgie, but not for any milk-and-water blood in your veins.'

Georgina looked warningly in Celine's direction, but William paid no attention at all. His eyes slid over her, their meaning perfectly plain to any observer, and then he turned round in his seat again, saying something *sotto voce* to Stuart that Georgina couldn't quite catch.

She was glad when they reached the Hindu temple and Rabahindre came running forward to meet them. He put the palms of his hands of his together and lifted them high in front of his face. 'We are all ready, madam,' he said to Georgina. 'Everyone is very pleased to have you visit us!'

And sure enough, it seemed as though the whole village had turned out to mark their arrival. The children stood in neat lines on one side of the open space in front of the temple, watching eagerly as the visitors were divested of their shoes and led into the first of the chambers inside. There they were met by the local priest, a member of the lowest of the Hindu castes as were his flock, dressed in a white garment that was already stained with the mud of the evening before.

Georgina's first discovery was that the concrete floor was

as slippery as glass. The roof had leaked in places, allowing the rain to come flooding in, and they were up to their ankles in muddy water long before they had passed through the outer room into the inner sanctuary.

The priest began a long sustained chant, the meaning of which had been lost in antiquity. Georgina remembered someone at college telling her that Hindu gods were some of the oldest in the world and that there was a school of thought that thought the gods of ancient Greece had originated from the same source, travelling to Europe by way of the very island where she was standing now.

The white-robed figure advanced towards them with a tin plate on which were mixed a number of coloured pastes. With infinite care he marked their foreheads and garlanded them with chains of marigolds and gold and silver decorations of the kind that we put on Christmas trees in England. Then with half a coconut in their hands, filled with flowers and the leaf of the betel-nut, they were led forward until they were almost touching the table that served as an altar and which stood in front of three curtained cubicles in which were hidden the representations of three of the most important members of the Hindu pantheon.

When the first curtain was drawn back, the elephant-headed son of Shiva and his consort, variously known as Parvati, Durga, Kali, etc., was revealed. Ganesha, as the remover of obstacles, is propitiated by every Hindu before every major undertaking and is much more popular than his warlike brother, Kartikeya, who is more generally known in South India by the name of Subrahmanya.

The central curtains revealed the more important god Shiva, the third member of the Hindu triad, the destroyer and the lord of the dance and who is sometimes worshipped for his sexual proclivities also. This last was brought home by a curious iron object on the altar in front of him that Georgina only belatedly recognised to be some kind of phallic symbol. Incense was burned before him and the chanting increased in intensity until one of the poorest-looking members of the congregation went off into a trance and began an erratic kind of dance that made Celine ask nervously, 'Is he all right?'

'It can happen to anyone,' Stuart reassured her. 'If he gets out of control, they'll touch him with some of the sacred ashes and he'll come out of it. It can happen to anyone. It could even happen to you.'

Happily, Celine had no time to express any further doubts before the priest was holding out a bowl of smouldering coals towards them and, following Stuart's example, they cupped the smoke into their hands and brought it up to their faces and down over their heads.

'What does this do?' Georgina asked in a whisper.

'You're receiving the power of the god,' William answered her.

She hoped it would work for a non-believer and doubled her cash contribution to the proceedings as a kind of insurance that it would. She knew little or nothing about Shiva, but she was attracted by his dancing figure with its many arms and one leg raised, while the other stood on some diminutive figure down below.

The children had crowded into the limited space behind them, their dark eyes large with curiosity and shining with the reflected light of the candles. They were beautiful, well-made children, much given to laughter and with all the curiosity about visitors that is universal among the less literate, who get their news by word of mouth rather than from the written word. It seemed to Georgina that there was no air at all left inside the temple and she began to hope the ceremony would soon come to an end.

When it did, it was with a suddenness that made her forget all about the slippery floor, and she very nearly fell as they turned and made their way outside again.

'The priest doesn't speak English,' Stuart warned her, so, as something was expected of her, she turned to Rabahindre and asked him to thank him for them.

'It was a great honour for us,' she insisted. 'I wouldn't want him to think us ungrateful. You will make sure that he understands that, while we're not Hindus ourselves, we're proud to have been allowed to visit his temple.'

Rabahindre grinned. 'He knows, madam. I have told him all about you and everyone is happy you came to see our gods. Now he has seen you for himself, he will allow you to see the demon as you asked. Excuse me, madam, if you will follow me, we will go now.'

He led the way through the pitiful houses of the lines where most of the workers on the estate lived. Children abounded, falling in and out of the puddles that had not yet dried out, and thoroughly enjoying the novelty of having these strangers among them. Yet they made little noise. No one cried out, as they would have done at home in England; they watched and giggled in almost total silence, nudging each other if anything of particular interest happened.

The masks and home-made dancing figures were kept in a shed at one end of the village. Rabahindre unlocked the rusty padlock on the door and, gesturing them to stay outside, went in himself and came out again carrying several highly coloured ancient masks in his arms.

'But they have no bodies!' Celine complained.

Rabahindre waggled his head. 'Not now, Miss Celine. Every year they have a new body specially made for them. They are made of palm leaves, plaited together, and are beautiful. But they last only a little time. These ones are not used at this time of year. They have their own festivals at other times.' He turned back to the shed with an unconsciously theatrical air. 'Now you will see Mahasona!'

There was a lengthy pause, disturbed only by the sounds of activity from within the shed, and then the mask that Georgina had seen the night before emerged from the battered door, rolling its eyes and opening and shutting its mouth, looking exactly as though it were indeed drinking the blood of the elephant's head that was raised again and again to its lips. Georgina found it hideous, the more so now that she could see the vivid colours in which it was painted: scarlet, green, yellow, and white, outlined in black. The body followed more slowly, its plaited shape catching in the light breeze and making it difficult to control. Finally it stood beside them, towering up into the sky, the result of many hours of work and startling in its evil aspect.

Georgina turned to Celine in time to see her normal pink and white complexion turn to a sickly green.

'Is that what you saw?' she demanded.

The younger girl put out a hand which was immediately captured by one of Stuart's. 'I can't look at it! Please, Georgina, don't make me look any more!'

'But is it the same?' Georgina insisted.

Celine closed her eyes and swayed in time to the gigantic figure in front of them. 'Take me away!' she pleaded to Stuart.

'But you haven't said if that's what you saw!' Georgina objected. She felt William's hand on her shoulder and tried to shake it off. 'Celine, you *must*——'

'Leave her alone, Georgie,' William bade her. 'Can't you see she's in no state to be asked anything now?'

'But——'

'Georgina, don't bully her now!'

Georgina turned outraged eyes on to him. 'I was not——'

He pushed her hair away from her face. 'You've made your point, sweetheart. I'll do the rest. Okay?'

She didn't know whether she would have given in to him or not, because at that moment her attention was diverted by some of the men from the village gently lowering the plaited figure to the ground and releasing an excited Rabahindre from underneath.

'Come closer, madam,' he invited Georgina. 'You can see now how clever this mask is, yes? Hold it here, and here, madam. Now you can work it too! Excuse me, madam, like this!'

Georgina tugged on the ropes as she was bidden and found the mask less revolting when she was in charge of its movements. Indeed, she was beginning to see the fascination of an art form that at first she had found shocking and rather frightening. It was very cleverly made, fitting together as beautifully as if it had been made with precision instruments rather than the adze and clumsy knife that were the tools of the village carpenter.

She pulled on another rope and the mask rolled its eyes with devastating effect. Celine uttered a scream of fright and hid her ashen face against Stuart's shoulder. 'Take me away!' she moaned.

He went with her without a backward glance. Georgina, beginning to enjoy herself, made the mask stick out its tongue at William, and she grinned at him happily.

'Isn't it clever?' she remarked. 'Do you want to work it?'

He shook his head. 'Aren't *you* clever!' he mocked her. 'It would seem you were right, if Celine ever recovers sufficiently to confirm the fact. And not only about that. She's cut you out with Stuart, my poppet, and I don't think he looks on her as a child either. What are you going to do about that?'

She returned the mask to Rabahindre, giving her husband an uncertain smile. 'Encourage it?' she suggested hopefully.

'You may be right.' He dug a few coins out of his pocket and handed them to Rabahindre.

'Of course I'm right!' She picked a few more coins out of his hand and added them to the pile on Rabahindre's palm, enjoying the intimate feeling it gave her. Indeed, she felt so comfortable with William at that moment that she completely forgot to guard her tongue and said impulsively, 'If only Jennifer doesn't upset everything when she comes!

I could almost wish that she's still on about you, but that would be too much to hope. She'll probably want both of you!'

'Celine has no reason to be jealous of your sister,' William rebuked her. 'I hope they'll be friends.'

Georgina's spirits sank. It was impossible for her to explain to William that Jennifer scorned to have friends of her own sex and that she certainly wouldn't have any time for Celine, except to try and belittle her shining beauty. She would have plenty of time for Stuart, though, and she wouldn't be happy until she had him dancing attention on her. Even if she had come for William, she would still want Stuart too; it was the way she was made. Georgina had long ago accepted the fact that she would never change and she had spent so many years protecting Jennifer from the consequences of her own actions that it was second nature to her now. Even the best juggler in the world would occasionally let a ball drop, and Georgina had been cast in the role of the assistant who picks it up and sets it spinning in the air again so often that she had never resented that all the applause for the act had always been reserved for Jennifer. It was only now that she had found someone even more vulnerable, who needed protecting far more than Jennifer ever had, that she knew that this time she couldn't allow Jennifer to purloin Stuart away from her. Jennifer played with men's hearts as if they were toys created especially for her pleasure, and Stuart would be no different from any of the others. But to Celine he was the one person in the world who could give her a normal life, putting the tragedy that had marred her life behind her for ever. *This time she couldn't allow Jennifer to do it!*

'I suppose she has to come?' she sighed.

'Why not?' he returned indifferently. 'It will be on your own head if she takes anything you value away from you, Georgie Porgie. You have no reason to be jealous of her unless you want to be.'

Miss Campbell was waiting for them back at the bungalow. She took one look at Celine's pale face and turned on Georgina.

'I told you she wouldn't be able to stand up to seeing that—*thing*! I hope you're satisfied now! I shouldn't be surprised if we have more than a few nightmares tonight! Come along, Celine. Say thank you to Mr Duffield for looking after you nicely. *He* wasn't to know that you aren't up to that kind of thing. We know whom to blame, don't we, dear?'

Celine clutched at Stuart's arm. 'I don't want to go with her!' she breathed, swallowing convulsively. 'I want to stay with you!'

'Oh, quite,' Stuart agreed, putting a matter-of-fact arm about her and hugging her in much the same way as he would have done a child. 'You can't go yet! You haven't told us if that was the same demon as the one you saw last night?' Celine shuddered visibly, but he went on speaking to her in the same calm tones. 'Georgina went to a lot of trouble to show you that it wasn't something in your own imagination which you saw. I think we ought to talk about it now, don't you?'

Celine's eyes were troubled, but there was none of the blankness of former times about them. 'Yes,' she said simply.

'Then you'd better sit down and tell us all about it.' Her fingers tightened on his shirt-sleeve. 'It's all right,' he soothed her. 'I'll be here.'

'Always?'

'As often as I can be. I can't always be with you, though. You'll have to get used to that. It won't matter, you know, once we've talked about it.'

'Won't it? You'll go on liking me——'

'Nothing could make me dislike you. You have my word on that.'

Apparently she believed him. 'It was the same demon,'

she said on a sigh. 'But it wasn't the same as the one I saw before. He always burst into flames. There was always fire everywhere, just as there was when Mother died. I liked fires before that. I had some matches and I was lighting them one by one. I may have started the fire that burned down the house.'

'Was the demon around before the fire?' William asked suddenly.

Celine's eyes never left Stuart's face, but they widened with fright as she made a conscious effort to remember the night her mother had died.

'Yes,' she said at last. 'Mother saw him too—I'd forgotten that. All these years I'd forgotten that! I tried to tell Father that he'd been there and that Mother was frightened of him, but he and Miss Campbell said I'd imagined him— that there never had been anything.'

'Interesting,' William commented.

Miss Campbell's hand shot out and she slapped Celine hard on either side of her face. 'You're as mischievous as your mother! She was always trying to turn your father away from me too!'

Stuart moved towards the hysterical woman, but William was even faster. 'I think we've heard enough,' he said, bundling Miss Campbell into the house before him. 'I'll take Miss Campbell into Nuwara Eliya straight away and put her in a hotel. The rest is best forgotten once Celine has got it out of her system. Georgina, you'll look after her until I get back, won't you?'

Georgina started and nodded. 'How long will you be?' she asked.

He turned and looked at her, but she couldn't read the expression in his eyes. 'Who knows?' he said.

'*Girls and boys, come out to play, The moon doth shine as bright as day.*'

Georgina could hear Celine's pretty young voice rising

and falling as she sang the old nursery rhyme to herself out on the verandah. But she had not been singing earlier; then she had been distressed and grey with fatigue.

'You can't possibly understand how it was,' she had said. 'You see, I've always thought I killed her. If I had, I wouldn't deserve any happiness, would I?'

'I don't know,' Stuart had murmured thoughtfully. 'Who gave you the matches to play with? I'd say the blame was largely theirs.'

Celine had responded with all the eagerness of a young puppy. 'But I can remember it all now!' she had exulted. 'I never did light any of the matches because I heard a funny, whirring noise. I looked out of the window and there was this black man with paint all over his body and he was whirling something round and round his head. Then everything went up in flames. I climbed out of the window and ran round to the front of the house, where Miss Campbell was standing. She was calling out something to the black man and he went inside the back door, but the fire must have come rushing out towards him when he opened the door, because I remember him being surrounded with flames—and he never came out again. I wanted to go inside to my mother, but Miss Campbell wouldn't let me go. She kept saying she was glad she was dead. It went round and round in my head until I thought I was saying it too.'

'I never did like Miss Campbell,' Georgina had said with distaste.

'No,' Stuart had agreed, 'but we'll never know now what her part in the fire was. Perhaps it's best that way.'

Celine had nodded decisively. 'Poor thing, she thought she would have Father all to herself, but all he wanted from her was a nurse for me. Funny, I might have hated her if we'd never left Australia, but now I know how she must have felt. Sometimes one can't make do with less than everything from a particular person. She should have gone away long ago.'

'And allowed you to grow up?' Stuart had said very gently.

Celine had looked at him, her heart in her eyes. 'I'll try,' she had said.

Stuart had gone away shortly after that. Georgina and Celine had waited for William until they were both rubbing their eyes to keep awake, it was so late. Georgina had insisted that they dined at their usual hour because there were the servants to consider, but still William hadn't come.

'You go to bed, Georgie,' Celine had suggested, after they had finished their coffee out on the verandah. She had stretched, holding her arms high above her head. 'I feel so much lighter! I'll wait up for William, shall I?'

Georgina had thought the younger girl might have wanted to speak to William on her own, so she had gone meekly to bed, but that had been a long time ago now. Celine began the nursery rhyme all over again, a note of irrepressible laughter in her voice.

'Do you like that one?' she asked when she had finished.

'It's not my favourite,' William answered her.

'No,' she agreed, 'but I know what is! *Georgie Porgie*——'

'Where is she?'

'She was tired. She went to bed.'

'Good idea! Off you go too, Pussycat! Oh, and Celine, don't worry about anything any more. It will all come right now.'

'With Stuart too?' And then, when William didn't answer, 'Georgie doesn't want him. She said she doesn't. Besides, she's married to you!'

Georgina craned to hear William's answer, but it was lost on the evening breeze. All she heard after that was Celine's footsteps in the hall as she went to her room and the sound of William locking up the french windows for the night.

He came into her room through the bathroom. She had

not expected him and she lay very still, half hoping he would go away again.

'Georgie?'

'Go away!' she said.

His laughter gave her a winded feeling, as if she had been hit hard in the solar plexus.

'Georgie, my love,' he said, 'you've done it again! All the way home I've been telling myself how pleased you'd be to please me, that there wouldn't be a word of argument from you, only a soft, gentle woman welcoming me home——'

Georgina sat up in a rush. 'You should have known better!' she began.

He sat down on the bed beside her. 'Will you always want to fight, my Georgie?'

She hugged her knees tightly, considering whether she should turn on the bedside light or not. If she did, she would be able to see him the better, but that went both ways and he might discover the traces of tears on her cheeks and draw his own conclusions. He had been gone so long! But she would much rather he didn't know how his absence had affected her.

'Georgina——'

'If you come any closer, I'll—I'll black your other eye for you, William Ayres!' she threatened.

She heard his breath catch. 'You can try!' he retorted. 'Because I'm coming a whole lot closer, Georgie Porgie. Move over!'

She stared at him through the darkness, her heart taking up a new and exotic rhythm within her. 'What happens if I don't?' she asked him.

He scooped her up into his arms and deposited her on the far side of the bed, holding her hands in one of his behind her back. 'I've waited for this moment for a long time,' he said, and his voice made her tremble much as his kisses had earlier. 'You're not going to spoil it for me, are you?'

She stopped struggling. 'William?' she said on a note of

wonder. 'Is there anything to spoil?'

She felt his laughter against her ribs and she gave way willingly before his questing hands. 'As if you didn't know,' he said softly. And he kissed her.

# CHAPTER TEN

Georgina felt as contented as a well-fed cat. It was bliss. For a week she had done nothing but purr with pleasure at the new turn in her relationship with William. What did it matter if he didn't love her? It seemed no more than an abstruse philosophical point when she lay in his arms at night, or when he looked at her in that certain way of his in the daytime and she knew he was remembering, just as she was, the delights of the passion that flared so easily between them.

Of course, it wouldn't always be like this. She knew that, but she wasn't going to think about it now. Soon William would be away all day working and she would have to pay more attention to Celine and her problems. And then there was Jennifer——

'If you screw up your face like that you'll get terrible wrinkles,' Celine broke in on her thoughts. 'Think pleasant thoughts if you want to be beautiful! I remember my mother saying that.'

'If she was anything like you she didn't have much to worry about!' Georgina remarked dryly.

Celine laughed. 'Well, she wasn't. She wasn't at all like me—I mean, she wasn't beautiful in any way. Her face was a jumble of features and her teeth were all crooked. But she was never without a man at her side. They all loved her, even Father, though she made no effort to be faithful to him. Beauty hasn't anything to do with it.'

To Georgina, this was heresy. 'Wait until you meet Jennifer,' she said on a sigh. 'She's not as lovely as you are, but she's well enough to have put me in the shade all my life.'

'Perhaps she has something else as well. *You* have. You're nice.'

Georgina was about to say that Jennifer was not nice, but she stopped herself in time. It wasn't fair to denigrate Jennifer behind her back, especially as she was going to stay with them for a visit. There was always the possibility that William would be right and she and Celine would take to one another and become friends. If that were true, it would be a pity if she were to spoil it.

'Niceness is rather dull,' she said instead. 'It would be rather fun to be a *femme fatale* for a week, or a day, and see what it felt like!'

Celine fluttered her lashes, a superior look on her face. 'You should know if anyone does! William doesn't hover round you because you're nice! I don't know how you did it, Georgie, but I'm awfully glad you did. He feels better about all women since you came along. He's much nicer to me even. I used to think he found me a drag all the time and, after a while, I couldn't say anything sensible to him at all.'

'Miss Campbell didn't help——'

'No,' Celine agreed, 'but someone like you would have coped with Miss Campbell long ago. You may wish you were beautiful, but you can't wish it half as much as I wish I were more forceful and determined. I admire you for that!'

Georgina was astonished. 'Nobody else does! I've had to live with the fact that I'm a bully for years now!'

'Since William labelled you as one?'

Georgina nodded. 'He still thinks I need watching. I don't mind as much as I did, but when Jennifer comes— *She* never lays down the law! She suggests things to people and, of course, they do whatever she wants them to.'

'Even William?'

'Especially William!'

William came out on to the verandah to join them, his

chest bared to the sun. He was already the colour of mahogany, which made his eyes seem lighter and the golden lights in them more obvious.

'There's a letter for you,' he said to Georgina, and dropped it casually into her lap. 'From Jennifer.' He watched her pick it up and examine the envelope for herself. 'You don't have to check, it's just as it left her fair hand. I haven't steamed it open to find out what secrets you and she are keeping from me!'

'Good,' said Georgina. 'You're learning—though Jennifer never shares any of her secrets with me.' She waved the letter in the air, unread. 'Do you want to see for yourself?'

'If I want to read it, you won't keep it from me,' he smiled at her. He sat down on a chair and waited. 'Tell me what she says,' he commanded.

Georgina's eyes slid over her sister's large, spidery writing. Jennifer thought large writing denoted a generous nature and she made no effort to confine herself to more than a couple of words on every line. It meant that what Georgina could have written on a single page was spread over half a dozen, the lines tip-tilted and running into one another. It was large, but it was by no means easy to read.

'She's coming up from Colombo in her own chauffeur-driven car, which Duncan has insisted on paying for. Naturally, he wants her to have the best because he's still very fond of her. She hopes she hasn't broken his heart as she knows what it's like to be parted from the one person in the world for her. Only Duncan is luckier than she, because she hasn't been stolen from him by another. It's doubly hard when someone one has loved and trusted all one's life stabs one in the back. Didn't Caesar say, *'Et tu, Brute?'* to his friend Brutus as he did the dirty deed? She knows just how he felt.'

William didn't move a muscle. Georgina looked at him over the top of the letter, wondering what he was thinking.

'She doesn't say exactly when she's arriving,' she went on, a nervous tremor in her voice that refused to be dismissed.

'I've never had much time for Caesar myself,' William said suddenly.

All Georgina's worst suspicions were aroused. He had to be trying to tell her something and she was too obtuse to know what it was! She thought hard about Julius Caesar, but all she knew about him didn't make him particularly lovable in her eyes either.

'Why not?' she asked.

'He played both ends against the middle. His wife had to be above suspicion to keep the Romans quiet at home while he went off and conquered Cleopatra to make himself master of Egypt.'

'He was a great man!' Georgina protested. 'One can't judge them by ordinary everyday standards!'

'What other standards would one use?' he asked reasonably. 'And, more to the point, when does the individual decide he's great enough to use these other standards?'

Georgina gave him a helpless look. 'I suppose he just knows. Besides, I've always heard it that he couldn't resist Cleopatra's exquisite beauty. He probably couldn't help himself!'

'How very convenient,' William drawled. 'Would you allow such an excuse from me, Georgie Porgie?'

She might have to, she thought, when Jennifer arrived. 'I'd try to understand,' she said aloud.

He opened his eyes and her own widened at the gold flash she saw in their depths. 'Don't expect me to be so broad-minded if you take off! I've got used to having you at my beck and call and that's the way I like it.'

Her heart jerked within her. 'But it might not always be enough,' she forced herself to say. 'I wasn't your first choice—I may not be your last. *She* may be somebody else!'

William smiled a self-satisfied grin. 'If she is, don't expect to know anything about her. You won't get away from me as easily as that! You, I shall have and hold till death do us part, no matter what pleasant diversions crop up along the way!'

But Jennifer would make sure she knew! Jennifer would enjoy telling her the details of her conquest and, whatever William might say now, Georgina was as sure as her sister was that it would be Jennifer who would win.

William sat forward suddenly, making Georgina jump. 'What mischief are you thinking up now, my sweet? I make my own decisions, Georgie Porgie, and I reserve the right to make most of yours for you too, so don't get carried away by your own sense of importance! I won't be bullied by you, and the only force of arms I recognise from you takes place in bed—and very nice too!' He stood up, pushing an errant lock of hair away from her face. 'Won't you ever be content to allow that in me you've met your master?'

If only it were as simple as that! 'I may still escape you,' she warned him.

The prospect didn't seem to worry him. 'Do you want to?' he challenged her.

Sometimes she did. Sometimes she wanted passionately to get away from him, but she hadn't wanted to in the last few days, and she was ashamed that he should know it too.

'I'm an ordinary healthy female,' she began. 'Most women like to be mastered in bed.'

His smile looked to her eyes to be wolfish and not very kind. 'We're not in bed now, Georgina, and I'm still your master!'

Celine blinked at them both and eased herself out of her chair, mumbling something about taking a walk across the tea gardens towards the bungalow where Stuart lived. 'Atta girl, Georgina!' she added over her shoulder, giving the clenched fist salute as she went. 'Give him all you've got!'

The colour swept up Georgina's face. '*Celine!*' she pleaded. 'Don't go!'

'I've already gone,' Celine answered. 'I may be a bit lacking, but at least I know when I'm not wanted. See you later!'

Georgina retired into a sulky silence, but when she saw that it was going to take much more than that to remove William from the strategic position he had chosen, standing over her and, at the same time, preventing her from leaving her chair, she rushed into speech.

'Now look what you've done!' she attacked him. 'If she's going to visit Stuart, I ought to go with her. She's quite capable of allowing him all sorts of liberties—in fact, she'll probably demand that he does——' She broke off, not quite knowing how to finish the sentence.

'Make love to her?' William ended it for her. 'Stuart will look after her better than you can, Georgie. Your place is here with me.'

'Until Jennifer comes——'

'If you feel like that, why didn't you write and tell her she couldn't come?'

She shrugged her shoulders. 'She'd have come anyway. She wants you back!'

'And are you going to give me back?'

She shrugged again. 'Why not? You were never mine anyway.'

'But you are mine, Georgie Porgie. What are you going to do about that?'

Tears pricked at the back of her eyes. 'What would you have me do? Bully the life out of her until she turns round and goes away? Jennifer never goes away. She's always there. She always has been!'

'I see. I hadn't you realised you felt like that about her——'

'You've always told me I was jealous of her and, you see,

you're quite right! She even has Duncan paying for her car!'

William's lips curved into a mocking smile. 'Do you want him to pay for one for you too?'

Her indignation knew no bounds. '*Duncan?* That creep? I wouldn't give him the time of day!'

'Then why the jealousy?' he pressed her. 'Aren't you satisfied yet that I want you quite as much as you want me? Has our life together lacked anything for you these last few days?'

She refused to answer directly. 'That isn't everything,' she said darkly. 'With Jennifer it wouldn't count at all!'

A distinct twinkle stirred the depths of William's golden eyes. 'We're talking about you, little Georgie. I got the impression it counted with you quite a lot.'

Incensed, she made a move to get past him, but he had her trapped. 'You didn't *ask* me, if you remember. I didn't have any choice in the matter. With you, I never do.'

'Exactly!' he encouraged her, just as if he were talking to a recalcitrant child. 'Between us, I'll always call the tune—in or out of bed! If you want me to turn my back on Jennifer, you'll have to be specially nice to me, my love.' He took her hands in his, unclenching her fists with fingers of steel. 'You wouldn't really try and black my eye again, would you?'

'Yes, I would!'

'No wonder Jennifer always gets there before you. She would scorn to use such tactics! I doubt she's ever made a boy cry in her life!'

Georgina's temper was stretched beyond endurance. 'What about Duncan?' she demanded crossly. 'Haven't you any sympathy for him?'

'Should I have?'

She sniffed. 'I'd have said you had a great deal in common! He's behaving better than you did, though. Next time Jennifer spurns you, William Ayres, don't expect me to mop your blood off the floor! I'll be busy elsewhere!'

'Not you, Georgie Porgie——'

'And don't call me that! When I'm free of you, I'll change my name to something different and forget all about your horrid nursery rhymes!'

He pulled her up into the circle of his arms, amused. 'You won't forget. It used to be Rowley-Powley before it was Georgie Porgie, and that could apply to any name. Besides, I like your brand of kisses and I like your name, my dear, and I like having you by my side. You'll never be free of me, Mrs. Ayres!'

He had some reason to be confident, she reflected dully, for she, too, doubted she would ever leave him until he decided to send her away. And Jennifer would see to that! She would never share any man she thought of as hers, not even with his wife!

His arms closed round her in a most satisfactory way. 'Be as tough as you like with anyone else, Georgie, but I know you better than that! You were never reluctant for me to have my way with you, and you're not reluctant to have me make love to you now.'

'You can't be sure of that!' she protested. She sounded breathless and pathetically eager. It was *his* fault! His hand searched out her curves and her heart turned over in anticipation of what would come next.

'Can't I? *Can't I*, Georgina?'

'It isn't love!' she burst out.

'Isn't it?' He laughed out loud. 'What do you call it? I won't believe you're still pretending to hate me. Are you, my sweet?'

'No.' She choked over the word, her hands covering his in a mute protest against their probing. 'William, we can't! Not here!'

His lips met hers, exploring her mouth with a thoroughness that deprived her of all further speech. She uttered a sob of pleasure and abandoned the attempt of trying to reason him into being more sensible. She felt herself lifted high up against his chest and wondered at his strength of arm. How dreadful that she should like being coerced by him! She ought to be made of sterner stuff, but she wasn't. She felt very feminine and deliciously weak, and it was the most marvellous sensation in the world.

He deposited her on the bed and stood back from her. 'What, no more arguments, Mrs Ayres?'

She spluttered with laughter, making no effort to move, not even when he knelt on the bed beside her and began to undress her. Only her eyes darkened with the strength of her emotions. 'I wish I were more beautiful for you,' she murmured against his hand, trying to impede its progress against her naked flesh. She shivered with pleasure as he defeated her ruse. 'Oh, William!' she breathed.

'Oh, Georgina!' he mocked her, his lips returning to her mouth. 'Confess now, my sweet, that you like it when I have my way with you. You do, don't you?'

'Yes!'

He paused in what he was doing, his eyes narrowing as he surveyed her. Then his lips met hers again in a kiss as soft as a butterfly's wings and she could feel his laughter against her breasts.

'How are the mighty fallen!' he taunted her. 'But it's not enough. Before I'm through with you, my darling, you'll weep with love for me, and then I'll have you just where I want you!'

William went to work the next day, and time hung heavy on Georgina's hands. She had wanted to go with him, to see how he went about the gigantic task of harnessing a whole river and deflecting its course away from the sea so that not a single drop of its precious fluid was lost to the land.

'Your job is to stay with Celine,' William had told her with a touch of severity. 'You can come to the site some other time.'

'I've got used to having you about,' Georgina had tried to

persuade him. 'What are Celine and I to do all day?'

'You could get Stuart to show you over the tea factory,' he had suggested.

'There'll still be tomorrow!'

He had given her an odd look then. 'I'm flattered,' he had said. 'I never thought you'd admit you could miss my company for a few hours.'

She had blushed scarlet, cross with herself for being so foolish as to betray her feelings to him. 'It's my pugnacious nature,' she had defended herself. 'I can't fight with Celine —it wouldn't do!'

The glint in his tawny eyes had discomfited her still further. 'I'll be back tonight,' he had said, and he had kissed her hard on the mouth, scattering her wits to the four winds. 'I'll see you then,' he had added, and she had been sure that it hadn't been entirely her imagination that he had been as much moved by the embrace as she, and she had been fiercely glad that he found as much pleasure in her body as she did in his.

Celine was in a bad mood too. She claimed she had a headache and retired to her bedroom, refusing to come out. At lunchtime, she looked tired and drawn, and Georgina began to worry in earnest about her.

'What's the matter?' she asked her bluntly. 'Is it Stuart?'

'I don't want to talk about it!' Celine retorted. For the first time since Miss Campbell's departure the blank look was back in her eyes and she made no effort to converse or eat, but sat in a withdrawn world of her own, refusing all Georgina's blandishments to make her pull out of it.

'I wish you'd tell me about it,' Georgina pleaded with her. 'I'm not feeling on the top of the world myself.'

A fleeting smile crossed Celine's face. 'Missing William already?'

Georgina nodded. 'I only fight with him when he's here,

but I can't settle to anything with him gone. Silly, isn't it?'

'You're in love with him,' Celine sighed. 'You're lucky!'

'Lucky!' Georgina stared at her. The tears came rushing into her eyes. 'He doesn't love me. He never will. He married me because he thought my sister Jennifer preferred someone else. He wanted to protect her from me!'

'Why?'

'He thinks I bully her into doing things she doesn't want to—that I broke up her romance with him. She wrote him a letter, you see, saying she'd changed her mind and wanted him after all. She gave it to me to give him on the plane, only inside it was written as if she'd wanted him to receive it before the wedding. If he'd had it then he wouldn't have married me.'

Celine shrugged. 'He doesn't seem to hold it against you. Anyway, why should you care? I wouldn't if I were married to Stuart. I wouldn't care about anything else.'

'Not with Jennifer on her way here?' Georgina said dryly.

Celine looked muddled and frowned. Georgina, looking up at that moment, caught her breath afresh at the younger girl's shining beauty, a beauty which was enhanced rather than otherwise by her supreme indifference to the effect it had on those about her.

'I always thought,' Celine began in puzzled tones, 'that everyone loved the people who are close to them. Everyone else, that is. I didn't love my mother, I hardly ever saw her. She was always out with some man or other. I loved Miss Campbell even less. I'm not sure about my father. I think I did love him—I liked him a lot when he had time for me. I've always felt guilty that I didn't love my mother and she died. But you don't love Jennifer, do you?'

Georgina had always pretended to herself that she did. 'I'm sure I do! I don't like her, but I'm sure I must love her!'

'Because she's your sister?'

'Well, yes,' Georgina admitted. 'I've never thought of doing anything else.'

Celine struggled within herself to find the words to explain something else she didn't understand. 'Stuart says I don't know how I feel about him either!' she blurted out. 'He's going to give me time to find my feet. Oh, Georgie, how can I all by myself? I've been alone so long!'

Georgina felt as helpless as her charge. 'Perhaps he's worried that you need someone, but not him in particular,' she suggested hopefully. 'You don't know many other men, after all.'

'I don't have to!' Celine maintained stubbornly. 'I want Stuart now. He says we both have to be free in case we find we prefer someone else, just as if his saying that makes any difference to how I feel about him. I'll never be free—even if I wanted to be! But he doesn't need me in the same way. He might find someone else and I think I'd die if he did!'

'Have you told him that?'

Celine shook her head. 'He may be afraid because I'm not—not *normal*. He wouldn't tell me so, though, would he? He wouldn't want to hurt my feelings. There must be hundreds of ordinary girls he could marry. I'm frightened he doesn't want me. That's why you're lucky to be married to William. You'll always be a part of him even if he does prefer your sister. I'd rather share Stuart than not have him at all.'

Georgina wondered if she could ever be as self-sacrificing, but she already knew that she couldn't. She wanted the whole loaf! For others half a loaf might be better than no bread at all, but it wasn't for her, not if Jennifer had the other half. Not if Jennifer had a single slice, come to that!

'I think you're completely normal,' she said aloud. 'And you have a much nicer nature than I have. I want what I want, much more than I want what William wants!'

For once Celine looked the older of the two. 'Because they're the same thing, Georgie. Otherwise you wouldn't. He can't want Jennifer very badly or he wouldn't have married you. I daresay he doesn't really love either of you, but he's married to you. I'd give anything to be married to Stuart!' And she began to look so miserable again that Georgina felt quite cheerful about her own chances with William by comparison. William would be coming home to her that evening and she could hardly wait. All would be well, she thought, just as long as William went on coming home. While he did that, they were a team, and the longer a team stayed in harness the more difficult it was to destroy the partnership.

The two girls decided to make Georgina a new dress after lunch. Celine had supplied the material, a beautiful *batik* cotton which she had bought for herself in Nuwara Eliya, but which she had afterwards had thought was too definite a colour for her fair beauty.

'I like it,' she said indifferently when Georgina said she should keep it for herself, 'but I'll never wear it. Not that shade of green with my hair!'

'Perhaps not,' Georgina decided. She couldn't help fingering the thick cotton to examine the pattern more closely. The amount of work that had gone into dyeing the pattern was frightening. She could imagine how long it had taken waxing the area that was not to be dyed any particular colour, and then waxing it again for the next colour, and so on until the whole design was complete. 'I'll get you another dress length when I go with William to the site. We learned to do this sort of thing in college, but I can't say my efforts were as fine as this.'

'You should see some of the wall-hangings!' Celine enthused. 'They're real works of art! I wanted to buy one, but Miss Campbell wouldn't let me. She doesn't like beautiful things.'

Georgina laughed. 'She's so terribly ugly herself, isn't

she? I mean not just ugly in a bearable way, but she's made herself ugly. Poor thing, one has to feel sorry for her for having to live with herself!'

Celine averted her face so that Georgina couldn't see her expression. 'I had to live with her for years. I still can't believe she's gone.' She hesitated. 'I don't believe she started the fire herself, you know, though William thinks she might have done. I think she made that man come and dance outside the window to frighten Mother, though. Afterwards she made him come again and frighten me. She'll never let me go if she can help it.'

Georgina felt a strange disquiet settle over her own spirits. 'William won't allow her to have anything more to do with you.'

'No,' Celine agreed. 'Not if he can help it. But if I were married to Stuart no one would have to keep her away, would they? I feel safe with Stuart.'

Georgina put out an impulsive hand, grasping the other girl's arm. 'She won't come back here, darling. William is a dangerous man when he's crossed—as I have reason to know! She wouldn't risk another brush with him.'

Celine shrugged off her hand, spreading the material on the floor of the sitting-room. 'She would, you know,' she said quietly. 'She has great faith in her own powers—and so have I!'

'Her powers?'

Celine twisted her lips into the semblance of a smile. 'She found out about them when she was a child. They work too. That's why she kept me alive, because one day I'd add to her powers. She was always telling me so. Otherwise I could have died with my mother and welcome!'

'But that's horrible!' Georgina protested, wondering if she or William would ever know what Celine had suffered at that terrible woman's hands.

'That's Miss Campbell,' said Celine.

The light was fading from the sky when the sound of a car coming up the drive made Georgina dash to the front door. She didn't care if William did laugh at her, she had to welcome him home in person and, besides, she wanted to tell him about Miss Campbell. But it was not the jeep that William was using that edged its way forward through the trees. This was a saloon car and it hooted at every bend in the way of every Sinhalese driver. A stunning disappointment welled up inside her. She had been so sure it would be William at last, and it wasn't. On the contrary, there was nobody else it could be but Jennifer.

The car drew up beside the front door and Georgina went out to meet her, forcing a smile of welcome on to her lips. Jennifer, elegant and imperious, emerged from the car and smoothed down her skirt with a much-ringed hand. She held up the rings beneath Georgina's nose and laughed.

'I bought them on the way here. Sapphires are two a penny out here and I never could resist them!'

Georgina felt at a loss. Her eyes gravitated to the car again just in time to see another figure getting out of the back on the far side.

'You're not alone?'

'No. Isn't it a giggle?' Jennifer giggled charmingly. 'Miss Campbell is my travelling companion while I'm in Sri Lanka. I found her all alone in Kandy and we decided to go on together.'

'I know Miss Campbell,' Georgina said huskily.

'That's right, she does,' Miss Campbell agreed complacently. 'I'm back, just like the proverbial bad penny! You can't keep a good man down, can you? And how are we getting on with my poor little Celine, Georgie Porgie— no, I have to say Mrs Ayres, don't I? Managed nicely without me, have you?'

Jennifer's tinkling laugh ran through the dusk of the evening. 'Oh, Georgie! Has that unfortunate rhyme followed you out here too? Shall I speak to William about it on your behalf?'

'No, thank you,' said Georgina, and she led the way, slowly and reluctantly, into the bungalow and the brightness of the electric lights.

# CHAPTER ELEVEN

Georgina's heart ached in sympathy when she saw William's weary, resigned face. 'I was hoping you'd be home earlier,' she said.

He pushed the curl off her forehead with an impatient hand. 'Don't start on me now, Georgie, there's a dear. It's been one hell of a day! I should have gone down there earlier and seen how things were going——'

'It hasn't been much of a day here either,' she interrupted him. 'Oh, William, Miss Campbell is here! Jennifer arrived too. Miss Campbell is her new travelling companion.'

'Is she, though? I can't say I admire her taste.'

'No,' she muttered darkly. 'And that isn't all! Jennifer *likes* her!'

Wiilliam gave her a look of exasperated amusement. 'If she didn't, she wouldn't have brought her with her. Oh well, I don't suppose it matters really, and quite honestly, at the moment I'm too tired to care about who we have in the house! I'll have something to eat and go straight to bed. Don't worry about disturbing me, my dear. I'll sleep in the other room.'

He couldn't have hurt her more if he had struck her. 'Must you?' she asked tremulously. 'I—I——'

'You don't have to pretend, Georgina. You'll be glad to have your bed to yourself for a night, won't you? It'd be different if we were going to make love, but I'm pooped. I could sleep for a week!'

Georgina threaded her fingers together in a nervous gesture. 'Is it always going to be like this?'

'I hope not!'

'It isn't because Jennifer is here?'

His eyes narrowed. 'How could it be? I haven't seen her yet. Come on, out with it! What's niggling you about Jennie now?'

Georgina gulped. 'I just thought——' She took a deep breath to give herself courage. 'She's here now. I just thought you might not want me because she's under the same roof.'

'Georgie dear, I'm tired! Haven't I given you sufficient proof this last week that I want you? Jennifer won't make any difference to that! But not tonight, sweetheart. Okay?'

She nodded, unconvinced. 'What am I to do about Miss Campbell?'

His irritation surfaced again. 'Does it matter? She won't be able to do much harm in a few hours, will she? I'll have a word with her before I leave for work tomorrow.'

Georgina's gaze caught and held him. 'I'm frightened of her,' she confessed. 'Celine says she has powers and that she'll never let her go because of them. I think I believe her.'

'Rubbish, sweetheart. What powers can she possibly have?'

'I don't know. But she said she'd be back and here she is!'

'Thanks to Jennifer!'

'Yes, but she managed to persuade her to bring her. Jennifer isn't very biddable about that sort of thing. She hasn't much time for her own sex at the best of times, but someone as ugly and unpleasant as Miss Campbell? How did she manage it?'

'Not by witchcraft! I expect Jennifer took pity on her *because* she's ugly and unfortunate in her manner. She always had a kind heart.'

Georgina compressed her lips into a straight line, telling herself it would be folly to pursue the matter further.

Besides, what did she expect William to do? He looked tireder than she had ever seen him, and her conscience smote her. He had his own worries, couldn't she cope with the ones that Miss Campbell's presence had brought them? What kind of a wife was she, anyhow, to badger him now when she could see for herself how exhausted he was?

'William——' He looked an enquiry. 'I'd rather you slept in my room with me. I won't bother you——'

But he shook his head. 'Nothing doing, my sweet. I know you better than that! Of course you'd bother me!' He laughed without any amusement. 'Get someone to bring me some sandwiches, will you? And keep Jennifer out of my hair until tomorrow. Can you do that?'

She looked down, veiling her eyes with her lashes. 'I'll bring you the sandwiches myself. Sleep well, William.'

He tipped up her face and kissed her on the lips. 'Thank you, Georgie. Could you believe they were using the wrong core to pack the base of that dam? It will all have to come out again. That'll teach me for allowing you to distract me from the task in hand!' He kissed her again. 'If you think it's hot up here, you should try a day out in the sun down there. No, on second thoughts, you'd better not. I like you cool and fresh and sweet-smelling! I must smell like a Turkish bath!'

She rubbed her hand against his chest, smiling. 'I don't mind,' she said. 'You could smell like a pig for all I care!'

He smiled genuinely then and delivered a slap on her behind. 'Who'd have thought you'd turn out to be such a sexy piece?' he teased her. 'See that you only show that side of yourself to me, Georgie Porgie, or it'll be you who sports the next black eye!'

'I'm not afraid!' she sang out, dancing out of his reach. 'Last time it was I who got through your defences! You never know when I might do so again!'

'Oh, Georgina!' He shook his head at her. 'What an appetite for doing battle you have! Don't you ever give up?

You must know by now that I'm the natural victor between us.'

She looked up at him, her eyes sparkling. 'Prove it,' she challenged him.

He took a step towards her. 'With pleasure! But not now, Georgie! You have our guests to consider, and I have some sleep to catch up on. But one day soon I'll make you cry uncle, and I'll enjoy every minute of it!'

She thought she would too, but not with Jennifer, the true love of his life, in the same house. Her pleasure in the cut and thrust between them fell away from her and thoughts of her sister and Miss Campbell came crowding back into her mind.

'I wish they hadn't come!' she said out loud.

His eyes were kind, but very, very tired. 'Cheer up, they won't stay for ever.' He turned away from her, going through the bathroom to his own bedroom. Halfway there, he turned and spoke again: 'Keep Celine out of Miss Campbell's way, won't you, Georgie? I couldn't stand her screaming her head off in the middle of the night to-night——'

'Then you do think she might get at her?' Georgina demanded.

'I think she may try if it's made easy enough for her. It's up to you to keep them apart. Jennifer will help you, if you explain things to her properly. She brought her here, after all!'

It was strange how obtuse the most intelligent of men could be, Georgina thought to herself, trying not to wince physically as he shut the door behind him. It did hurt, though. She had been looking forward to his homecoming all day, longing for his company, and now to be deprived of it made her want to cry. Nor were Jennifer and Miss Campbell the substitutes she would have chosen to sit opposite her at the dinner table. And what about Celine? Could she be persuaded to have her meal in her room?

Georgina sighed, deciding that wouldn't do either. She had to see Miss Campbell some time if she was staying in the same house; it might as well be in company, when Jennifer and she were there to protect her.

When she went in search of the younger girl, however, she was nowhere to be found. Only Jennifer was in the sitting-room, smoking a cigarette in one of the longest holders Georgina had ever seen. This was a new affectation and one that wouldn't last long, judging by the ham-fisted way Jennifer chose to wield it, swirling it about her head.

'Aren't I to be allowed to see William?' she greeted Georgina in her usual sarcastic style. She seldom bothered to charm her own family unless she wanted something from them.

'Not tonight. He started work today and things haven't been going well without him. He's very tired and he's gone straight to bed.'

'How boring!'

Georgina kept a stern check on her temper. 'He came out here to work,' she said mildly. 'He likes these Commonwealth projects and he wants it to be a success.'

'More likely it's a good excuse to get away from you, Georgie. All men get tired of fighting with you sooner or later, don't they? I could name quite a few who turned from you to me with obvious relief. You never learn, do you, my pet?'

'You were welcome to all of them,' Georgina replied mildly.

'And William?'

'I'm married to William.'

'But for how long? You don't flatter yourself that you'll be able to keep him, do you?' She looked smug. 'Didn't you guess that I came out here to retrieve my property from your ungentle hands? I want William, and I'm going to have him. I made a mistake sending you to tell him about Duncan. I thought he'd give you beans for your trouble, not marry you instead of me! Why didn't he? Not that it matters! He won't stay with you for a moment longer than he has to, not when he knows that I'm available. He's in love with *me*, remember?'

Georgina tried to keep calm. 'I wonder if he is,' she observed. 'He doesn't seem overjoyed by your arrival, does he?'

'Only because he's afraid of what will happen when we meet,' Jennifer claimed with such certainty that Georgina could feel herself being pushed into believing her. She wished she had a similar confidence in herself to sustain her.

She changed the subject. 'Did you know Miss Campbell used to look after William's ward, Celine?' she asked.

'Oh yes. She told me at once. You weren't very clever there, my dear Georgie. She considers you an enemy, and the Miss Campbells of this world know how to deal with their enemies.'

'Nonsense!'

'What about Celine's mother? I wouldn't be in your shoes for anything! You put an end to her nice comfortable job with Celine, didn't you? And she needed that girl——'

'Did she say as much?' Georgina was startled into asking.

'More or less. She came over to me in the hotel at Kandy and asked if I was any relation of yours. I can't say I was flattered at the likeness she thought she could see between us, but she has uncanny ways and she said she could see some kind of thread running between us. I thought it would be amusing to watch her at work on you—she's a very determined lady!—and I owed you a bad turn for taking William away from me. Poor Georgie! Life is going to be very unpleasant for you in the next few days, Miss Campbell and I will see to that!'

'It's not me I'm worrying about, it's Celine,' Georgina told her. 'That woman——'

'How noble you are! But then you always were. Did you marry William in order to protect me from his wrath over Duncan? It would be just like you! You never would have made Duncan cry if he hadn't been pinching my arm. I suppose William's black eye was like inspired! What have you found to quarrel with him about when I wasn't here to provoke you both? How dull you must have been!'

'We managed.'

Jennifer's eyebrows rose in disdain. 'In separate bedrooms? *Not* my idea of managing a marriage, I must say!'

Georgina swallowed down her anger. Her sister must have been very busy to have found out so much about the geography of the bungalow so quickly.

'Think what you like,' she said. 'William has old-fashioned ideas about marriage and I don't see yours appealing to him much. You'll have to settle for something less, Jennie, if you can.'

Jennifer was languidly amused. 'Become his mistress? Would you hate that very much? Yes, I can see you would. Have you fallen in love with William, Georgie? Was all that hatred just a pretence because he so obviously preferred me? He'll never love you, my dear. He loves me and he always has! I'll see to it he doesn't change his mind at this point in your favour, you can be sure of that. I always have been able to twist your men round my little finger. It's laughable that you still have lingering hopes of winning against me—and with William too! William will come to hell when I whistle to him, just like all the others, and you'll be left on the sidelines, which is where you belong! God, how I hate that holier-than-thou expression of yours! In fact, I don't like anything about you much. Nor does Mother. She dutifully sent her love, by the way, and said she hoped you were going to be sensible and not thwart your little sister's wishes——'

'And Father?' Georgina interrupted her.

Jennifer's smile was both malicious and contemptuous.

'Who cares what Father thinks? He didn't even send his love to you. He thinks fools ought to be made to suffer for their folly, and he thinks you a fool for inviting me to visit you. I do too.'

Georgina had never thought she would be glad to see Miss Campbell come into the room, but on this occasion she was. She patted one of the chairs, inviting the woman to sit down and asked her if she would like to have a drink before dinner.

'It's still arrack or nothing,' she told her, 'but the passion fruit juice is strong and cold.'

'I hope you haven't been allowing Celine to imbibe alcoholic drinks,' Miss Campbell reproved her. 'It won't do her any good. Little girls should be seen and not heard!'

Georgina eyed her thoughtfully. 'Celine has been very well this last week,' she said. 'She's all right now that she's remembered what happened when her mother died. It won't be easy to make a child of her again, I'm glad to say. She's not a little girl any longer, but a beautiful young woman.'

Miss Campbell turned a mottled red, her jowls shaking with anger. 'How clever we think we are! But pride goes before a fall, Georgie Porgie, and I for one won't lift a finger to save you when you topple over!'

'Nor I!' Jennifer drawled. 'For once, being right won't do you any good,' she gloated. 'I'll have William and I'll make sure you know all about it! You've always thought you were above being jealous of me, haven't you? You'll learn better!'

Georgina bit her lip, trying to strengthen her resolution to pay no attention to her sister's barbs. But she couldn't hide the pain in her eyes as the door opened again. She expected to see Celine, and she admitted to a certain curiosity as to what would be her sister's reaction to anyone as beautiful as she was, but it was not Celine who walked through the door: it was William.

'Hullo, Jennifer,' he said easily. 'Miss Campbell.'

Jennifer looked up at him through her lashes. 'Is that the best you can do, my Billy boy? Don't you dare kiss me with your wife looking on?' She giggled. 'Are you afraid she'll beat you up?'

'No to all that,' he answered shortly. He turned to Georgina, putting a hand on her shoulder. 'Have you seen Celine?'

'No, not since tea-time. Do you want her for something?'

'It doesn't matter. I rang through to Stuart—to tell him about things here—and he wanted to come over. I said I thought it better that Celine should go over there. She isn't in her room.'

Georgina rose to her feet. 'I'll go and look for her. Go back to bed, William. She'll be all right.'

A smile twisted his lips. 'Will you be all right too?'

'Of course.'

His hand closed over the nape of her neck. 'I'll come with you. Stuart is waiting for us by the factory.'

'What a fuss!' Jennifer chimed in. 'Who cares what's happened to her? We can manage very well without her——'

'No, I can't!' Georgina cut her off, her voice gruff with the effort of keeping her temper. 'She's the most beautiful creature imaginable and I'd never forgive myself if anything happened to her.'

'Of course not,' Jennifer mocked her. 'Let's hope she appreciates your efforts to keep her tied to your apron strings more than I did!' She became aware of William's incredulous gaze and blushed becomingly. 'Well, you know what Georgie is! She never thought anyone was good enough for her darling sister, who always had to be whiter than white. She bullied me shamefully! She probably bullies the unfortunate Celine too.'

Miss Campbell laughed. The sound of it echoed round the room, freezing Georgina's blood. 'So you've lost my pretty Celine, have you? Am I invited to come and look for her too?'

Georgina saw her sister flash some kind of message to the older woman, but Miss Campbell was not looking at either of them. Her eyes were on William, cold and starting out of her head. 'You thought you could stop me seeing her, didn't you? But you're too late! You're much too late! Jennifer and I saw to that!'

'*Jennifer!*' Georgina didn't recognise her own voice as she reiterated her sister's name. 'What have you done? Where is she?'

'I didn't do anything,' Jennifer protested, pouting sulkily in William's direction. 'We did run into someone on the way here, but I had nothing to do with it. Miss Campbell took her away somewhere. *I was glad she did!* Georgina might not care about other people being lovelier than she is, but I do! What a fuss about nothing! She won't come to any harm where she is.'

Georgina ran forward in her agitation, but William was before her. He slapped Jennifer lightly first on one cheek and then on the other. 'Hysterical female!' he muttered. 'Where is she, Jennifer? Or do you want some more of the same?'

'She's *not* hysterical!' Georgina flung at him. 'William, if you hit her again, I'll—I'll——'

He took a firm hold on Jennifer's hair, holding up his arm to fend Georgina away from them both. As she straightened her back, determined to make him loose his grasp, she saw that he was laughing at her and tried the harder to get a good blow in before he should take her challenge seriously and, inevitably, would defeat her intention.

'Yes? What will you do?' He took the full force of her fist on his open palm. 'I'm only doing what you should have done a long time ago! You don't have to fight *me* on her behalf, Georgie Porgie, not any more. You can settle with me afterwards when we have Celine back safe and sound.'

'But, William, Jennifer came here to be with you, and if you're in love with her——'

'I thought she'd be good for Celine!' He released his hold on Jennifer, staring at his wife. 'Georgie, I thought you *knew*——'

'Georgie never knows anything to her own advantage,' Jennifer said nastily. 'I don't know where your beastly Sleeping Beauty is, and I don't care!'

'Sleeping Beauty is my name for her,' Miss Campbell said quietly. 'Such a good name, don't you think? You won't find her, Mr Ayres. You're not the right Prince for her, being a married man, and Mr Duffield doesn't understand her. Nobody understands her as well as her Miss Campbell does! She'll sleep for a hundred years and give her youth to me——'

'My God! What have you done to her?'

'Nothing as yet. But you won't find her. Not even your clever little wife will find her now.'

Georgina turned to face her, catching a flicker of uncertainty in the pale, bloodshot eyes. For an instant she couldn't believe it to be true, but she knew that Miss Campbell feared her in some extraordinary way, and she pressed home her advantage with a ruthlessness she hadn't known she possessed.

'Oh yes, I'll find her. Your power is broken, Miss Campbell. Celine is mine!'

'We'll see!' Miss Campbell said grandly, but her fear was obvious now and they could all see it written clearly on her mottled, angry face.

Georgina took one look and shut her eyes to close out the sight. She felt William's arm close about her and shivered against him.

'We'd better go and get her,' she said.

'The villagers won't let you in.'

Georgina opened her eyes again. 'You think not? Rabahindre will talk to them for me.' Her fingers clutched at

William's shirt-sleeves. 'I know where she is,' she breathed. 'She's in that shed where all the masks are kept.'

Miss Campbell crumpled before them. 'I must get away!' she shrieked. 'I must go now!'

'That seems a very good idea,' William agreed. 'I'm sure Jennifer will lend you her car and chauffeur to take you back to Kandy, and this time, Miss Campbell, I suggest you don't come back.'

'Her father owed me the girl's life! With his wife gone, why didn't he marry me as he promised to do? But no, he gave me Celine instead—and now *she* has taken her away from me!' She broke into laboured sobs, making little rushes towards the door.

'Shall I see her off?' Jennifer asked of no one in particular. 'I suppose I ought to offer to go with her? Well, Georgina?'

Georgina chewed on her lip. 'Wh-what?' she stammered.

Jennifer sighed dramatically. 'You know why I brought her here. You know why I came myself. Are you going to let me stay, knowing all that, or are you going to behave like anyone else would do and chase me away, never to darken your door again?'

Georgina stared at her, and then she looked at William, silently pleading for his help. It seemed she only wanted what he wanted after all.

'Georgina is more gallant than either of us,' he stated at last, smiling wryly at his wife and sister-in-law. 'No doubt she'll face up to your presence with her usual courage, but not until I've had something of my own to say on the subject. Is Celine in that shed, Jennifer?'

Jennifer shrugged. 'I don't know. All I know is this girl came walking down the drive towards us and I wondered who she was. I mean, you don't see anyone as lovely as she is every day of your life, do you? Well, Miss Campbell saw her too, and she got out of the car and spoke to her. The girl seemed to go into a trance. Miss Campbell told me to wait in the car until she got back and I did. She was only gone a few minutes. Then she got back into the car and we came on here.' She gave William a shaken look. 'What is she? Some kind of witch?'

'She thinks she is. I don't believe it myself, but Georgie thinks she might be one, don't you, darling?'

Georgina swallowed, bemused. 'It doesn't matter now her power is broken. She's a sad person, isn't she?'

Jennifer cast her eyes up to heaven. 'It isn't true! Georgie, you can't feel responsible for her too! No wonder I've disliked you for years! You never give up on anyone, do you?'

'In your case, I'd say just as well,' William put in dryly. 'You wouldn't have got very far without her. How did your mother put it? You have so few friends of your own and Georgie's never come to the house when she's away. I've learned a lot about Georgie in the last few days—and a lot about you too!'

Jennifer decided to make the best of a bad job. She smiled winningly at them both, and shrugged her shoulders. 'Win a few, lose a few,' she drawled. 'What are we going to do now?'

William was very much in command of the situation. 'You're going to stay here,' he ordered Jennifer. 'Georgie and I will go and fetch Celine home. And, Jennie, if you want to stay, don't make more of a nuisance of yourself than you can help. Okay?'

'Okay,' Jennifer shrugged, accepting this diktat with a complacent smile. Georgina, who had constantly been astounded by her thick skin in the past, envied her her ability to make the best of things no matter how they turned out, and began to wonder what the morrow would bring for herself. William hadn't sounded at all lover-like when he had been addressing Jennifer just now.

'Are you coming or not?'

Georgina started, realising that he must have spoken

before but she had been too busy dreaming to listen to him.
'Of course I'm coming! Celine will need me—imagine
being shut into that shed for hours. William, you don't
think——'

'No, I don't,' he said with comfortable certainty. 'Celine
is used to Miss Campbell's ways. She's had to cope too
often in the past not to do so now.'

'It wasn't much of a life,' Georgina mourned. 'I hope
Stuart realises that!'

William's face relaxed into an indulgent smile. 'I'm sure
you'll tell him if he doesn't, my little Amazon. He won't
dare treat her badly with you around to put him right.'

Georgina's gaze swept upwards over his face. His eyes
were amused and shone like liquid amber with some other
emotion as well. Her heart went into some swooping acro-
batics that made it difficult for her to breathe.

'You ought to be in bed,' she told him. He looked
completely exhausted. 'I thought you wanted a good night's
sleep.'

'So I shall, once we've got Celine back safe and sound. If
she's at all nervous, she can share your bed tonight, and
then neither of you will feel lonely.'

'But, William——'

'Come on, love. Tomorrow is another day!'

And he would be working! She checked the rising hope
within her that he might have other plans of his own—plans
that would include her!—and tried to concentrate on the
matter in hand.

It was easier to do that once they were outside and there
was only the light of the waning moon to guide them along
the narrow path towards the village. They had to go past
the factory to get there and Georgina went running ahead,
calling Stuart's name as she went.

'We're here!' Celine's voice answered her. 'Georgie, is
that you? Oh, Georgie, I knew you would come! And
Stuart came too! He fetched Rabahindre with the key of

the shed and let me out. I don't know when I've been so happy!'

The two girls flung their arms round each other. 'She's gone, Celine, and this time she won't be back. You'll never see her again!'

Celine choked with emotion. 'I'm *glad* she came! It doesn't matter what she did in the past, this time it all came right! William said it would, but I didn't believe him then. I do now! Stuart won't let anyone look after me now except himself, not even you—isn't that wonderful? Oh, and Georgie, he doesn't *care* that I'm not very bright and all that. He thinks I'm beautiful!' She paused to allow this remarkable fact to sink in, quite unconscious of her listeners' united reaction.

'But, Celine, we all know you're beautiful,' Georgina said at last, almost humbly.

'Oh yes, *that*!' Celine dismissed her loveliness without interest. 'But Stuart thinks I'm a beautiful woman, not a thing to be looked at. That makes all the difference, you see. Oh, Georgie, I"m so happy I could burst!'

Stuart retrieved her from Georgina's embrace, making no more than a half-hearted attempt to put everything on a more normal footing. 'She's trying to tell you that we intend to get married,' he muttered to William. 'With or without your permission,' he added with a grin. 'I was going to wait until she'd seen a bit more of life, but this last incident has convinced me she's seen more than enough! What she needs is a loving, stable background.'

William shook his extended hand with vigour. 'I couldn't agree with you more! Do what you like with her. *I*'m going back to bed!'

# CHAPTER TWELVE

'I thought it might be a good time to take you over the tea factory,' Stuart suggested.

Georgina tried to look enthusiastic. 'Why not?' Why not, indeed? she added to herself. It would be hours and hours before William would be home. He could have looked in and wished her good morning before he had gone, but he hadn't, and by the time she had decided he was not coming and had hurried into her clothes in case she might be in time to have breakfast with him, he was already long gone.

'Jennifer might enjoy it,' Georgina forced herself to add. 'She ought to see as much as she can while she's here.'

Stuart's eyes flickered. 'How long is she staying?'

'Until she decides to go, I suppose.'

Georgina sounded so dispirited that Celine was concerned for her. 'Surely she won't stay now?' she exclaimed.

It was unfortunate that Jennifer should choose that moment to saunter out into the garden to join them. It was the first time she had seen Celine in the full light of day and the look in her eyes was far from being one of unmixed admiration.

'You must be Celine. Well, you don't have to worry, I wouldn't stay anywhere with you around! Very bad for the morale! And, since you're all too shy to ask me, my morale is sagging badly at the moment without having to listen to you telling me how *de trop* I am to *dear* Georgina's perfect marriage! I'll go as soon as my car gets back.' She smiled wryly at Celine's bewildered stare. 'You have to admit I was useful there! How else would you have got rid of the old harridan?'

'She wouldn't have been here,' Celine answered with a

logic Jennifer was far from appreciating. Her usual sunny smile broke across her perfect features. 'I'm glad she was, though. Stuart says we can get married at once now.'

'Stuart?' Jennifer's whole aspect changed at the prospect of meeting a man and not having to make do only with members of her own sex. 'Were you here last night?'

Stuart smiled briefly. 'I was outside.'

Jennifer took a step nearer to him, her whole being concentrated on his lightest word. 'How wonderful!' she breathed. 'I hope Celine knows how lucky she was to have you rescue her? I quite thought that that little enterprise was going to be left to Georgie. My sister, you know, thrives on manipulating people in and out of incidents of her creation. She has a chronic need to look after everyone all round her. Only there's a snag. There always is a snag, isn't there? Everything has to be done in the way she thinks will be best for you! Take care she doesn't make you out to Celine to be some kind of medicine she has to take three times a day to keep her nerves under control. Romance and nasty medicine don't go well together—and I can see you're romantic just by looking at you! One romantic can always spot another, can't they?'

Celine's lovely smile changed to stony displeasure. 'It isn't my nerves, there's nothing wrong with my nerves! I'm not very clever and I have bad dreams, but if Stuart doesn't mind, why should you?'

Georgina thought it was time she took a hand in the conversation herself, dragging herself away from her own attack of the miseries to deal with her sister. How Jennifer loved stirring things up with her little wooden spoon! But she wasn't going to spoil Celine's happiness, not if she, Georgina, could prevent it.

'Jennifer, don't!' she rapped out.

Her sister turned innocent eyes in her direction. 'Don't what?'

But it was Stuart who answered. 'I've heard a lot about

you, Miss Perry,' he said quietly, 'not from Georgina, but from William. He always said you had soft, gentle manners and a nice nature. Pity he was mistaken.'

Jennifer gasped. 'What do you mean?'

'I mean Georgina has had a lot to put up with from you in the past, but you won't have her around in the future to smooth your path for you. Shall I hand you a good laugh, Jennifer? Georgie gave your letter to William on the plane as you told her to. Anyone else would have torn it up unread, but not Georgina Ayres! William was furious, as you hoped he would be, but after a while he began to think there was more to it than Georgina hanging on to it until it was too late for him to do anything about it. He decided Georgie was the one who was telling the truth.'

'He never said so to me!' Georgina blurted out.

'He will, when he gets around to it,' Stuart said comfortably. 'Meanwhile, shall we go across to the factory?'

It was a subdued party that made its way along the path towards the factory. Stuart ignored their sulky faces and insisted they paid attention as he plucked a twig from one of the tea bushes and showed them how the white flowers grew underneath the leaves, facing down towards the ground.

'This is the bit which is picked,' he went on. 'Two leaves and a bud, never more than that. That's what those women are doing over there.'

He led them on into the factory, ignoring Jennifer's cries that she didn't want to go up the rickety steps that led to the upper storey of the factory.

'This is where the leaves are put to dry,' he explained, pointing to the long racks that stretched their way across the room. 'There's a complicated system of air vents that help desiccate them. One of my jobs is to see that they're not left here too long, or for too short a time. After that, the leaves are passed through these rollers——' he pointed out the giant, electrically operated machines—'and a chemical change begins to take place. Oxygen combines with the aromatic juices which are released and fermentation begins. The leaves change colour from green to copper and it takes judgment to know exactly when they are "done". The final stage is the firing, which arrests any further oxidization by baking the tea evenly. It depends where the tea is to be marketed as to how much firing we do in the factory. If it has to travel through the Red Sea, for example, it would get a further baking there, and that has to be allowed for.'

He rushed them round the building, going rapidly from one process to another, until they came to the place where he did the most difficult part of his work, the tasting area.

'Teas have such lovely names!' he enthused, putting the kettle on to boil. 'Pekoe, Orange Pekoe, Pekoe Souchong, Tippy and Flowery, among others. When you taste them you should be able to tell the major differences between them for yourselves.'

Georgina took the cup of tea he handed her and sipped it carefully. 'Is this a good tea?' she asked him.

'One of the best. Try this and you'll see the difference.'

She did and, even to her indifferent palate, it tasted rougher and more bitter than the first tea. 'Are there many different grades?' she pressed him, her interest now thoroughly caught.

He grinned. 'How about pungent, malty, pointy, bakey, thick, coppery, dull or bright? We tasters have our own jargon to describe every kind of tea. How would you like the job?'

He looked over her head as the sound of shod feet came through one of the open doors. 'At last!' he exclaimed. His smile widened as William joined them. 'I thought you were never coming! Pity, though, you're going to remove my star talent from our tea-tasting competition. I suppose you won't wait for her to finish the course?'

'Not today,' said William. 'She'll have to come back some other time.'

Georgina clasped her hands together. 'Shouldn't you be working?' she squeaked. She cleared her throat, and her voice came down a whole octave. 'I didn't expect you for ages!'

'I've been working! Good God, woman, I've been working since dawn to hurry things on and get back to you, and you don't even look pleased to see me!'

Georgina's eyes fell before his. 'I am—of course I am. Only you couldn't even be bothered to wish me good morning, so how am I expected to greet you now?'

William sighed. 'That's my Georgina! How about with a kiss?'

But Georgina couldn't, not with Jennifer standing there watching her, ready to pick holes in her performance. 'Not now!' she said urgently.

He appeared to find that riotously funny and her anger against him kindled into a steady blaze. '*Very* funny!' she jeered at him. 'But you've yet to prove to me that you want my kisses!'

His laughter fell away from him. 'That's true.' His tawny eyes challenged hers, making her feel quite dizzy with their impact. 'But if you think I'm going to do that in front of witnesses, you have another think coming. Some things are better done in privacy——'

'Because you're ashamed of me!' Georgina flung at him. His lips twitched. 'I want to spare your blushes——'

'You could have fooled me!'

'—but that isn't the same thing at all,' he went on calmly. 'That's because I don't want others to think I married anyone as stupid as you seem determined to be.' He shook his head at her. 'Really, Georgina, don't you ever think things out before you come rushing out of your corner, ready to do battle with all and sundry? Well, you're not fighting with me, my girl! Not today! Today you're going to learn what it means to be a wife——'

She panicked. 'I won't come with you!'

The golden flecks shone bright in his eyes. 'Won't you, Georgie? Why not?'

'Because——' she floundered. 'Because I don't want to!'

The gold flecks changed to warm laughter. 'You have a lot to learn, little Georgie, and I'm the man to teach it to you. Give in gracefully and come along, my love, because you're coming whether you want it or not, and you know it!'

If she ran, she thought, if she ran hard enough, she could still make her escape through the open door. But what would she do then? She eyed him with all the nervousness of a trapped animal and saw the purpose with which he in turn was regarding her.

'You can't carry me the whole way back to the house!' she declared with a lift to her chin.

'I won't have to!'

Georgina cast a proud, angry look about her, but there was no help to be gained from either Celine or Stuart, who were intent only on each other, and from Jennifer she would scorn to ask so much as the time of day!

'Where are we going, then?' she asked abruptly, knowing herself to be defeated.

'On a picnic,' he answered without hesitation. 'I have all the food in the jeep, waiting for you. Are you coming?'

She put her hand in the one he held out to her and bent her head. 'But I haven't forgiven you yet, William Ayres, not for anything!'

'Ah!' His fingers closed about hers with a painful intensity. 'It isn't your forgiveness I'm seeking,' he mocked her. 'I've never fancied the role of penitential sinner much and I won't grovel at your feet, because neither of us would care for that. I have another proposition to put to you——'

'And I suppose if I don't accept it at once, you'll coerce me into it just the same!' she interrupted him shortly.

'Why can't you be nice to me, just for once, just until— until——?' Her eyes widened and she stood stock still, refusing to budge another inch. 'William, what kind of proposition?'

'Why don't you come and find out?'

She blinked nervously. 'Will I like it?' she probed.

'You will, if you don't strain my patience too far before we get started! Look, sweetheart, I want you to myself for a few hours and I've spent a sleepless night and a great many hours of hard work to achieve it. Don't you think it's time we had a talk, just the two of us, without any interruptions, and got certain things straight between us?'

She nodded slowly. 'Didn't you go back to bed last night?'

'For a few hours.'

'Was that enough for you?'

His smile was wry. 'Lack of sleep doesn't help my temper any. You have been warned, my sweet Georgina! I need you on my side for the rest of today!'

'Oh yes!' she exclaimed. 'Why didn't you say so? I thought——' She broke off, wondering exactly what it was that she had thought. A proposition in her experience was the first step on the road to ruin, but as she was already married to William he couldn't possibly have meant the temporary liaison that his words had conjured up. Indeed, it had to be something else, and that something set her nerves jangling and the blood racing through her veins.

She ignored his look of enquiry, a smile of sheer delight hovering at the corners of her mouth. 'William, I wish you'd come earlier! It was such a long morning without you! Why didn't you come in to wish me good morning?'

'How do you know I didn't? You were fast asleep when I left the house this morning.'

'I wouldn't have minded if you had woken me,' she protested. 'I thought it was because you preferred to have breakfast with Jennifer.'

He cast a quick look in her direction, giving her a push towards his waiting jeep. 'Jennifer is essentially an evening person, don't you think?' he returned.

'I'd much rather you didn't think of her as any sort of person,' she said in a small voice. 'I know you thought you were in love with her——'

'That was a misunderstanding, Georgina. That's one of the things I want to talk to you about. I've treated you very badly, dear heart, but a little bit of it was your own fault. You're going to have to give up fighting me in the future and try a spot of loving instead. Think you can stand it?'

She sat on the canvas-covered seat, her knees together and her hands clasped lightly in her lap. The colour edged up her face as she strove to find a credible answer that would not commit her to more than he wanted from her. None occurred to her.

'Never mind, Georgie Porgie, I can wait.' He got into the driving seat beside her, lifting a hand in salute to the others who had come out from the factory to see them off. He grinned happily to himself. 'Atta girl, Georgie! At least Celine knows what she wants from Stuart!'

The tea gardens looked particularly lovely that morning. The atmosphere was thin and clear and it was possible to look across miles and miles of tea-planted hillsides and up into the heights where even the tea came to an end, to be replaced by some scrawny laurels, rhododendrons, pipal, balsams and pitcher plants. The land was well watered too, a multitude of waterfalls giving life to some of the rockier gorges.

Georgina was beginning to relax and enjoy herself. She knew what she wanted too. She wanted William, but she wanted him all to herself and, for today at least, that was what it seemed she was going to get.

'This must be the most beautiful place on earth!' she said, increasingly certain that this was going to be the most wonderful day in her life.

'It must be the company you're keeping,' he teased her.

She sat up very straight. 'Could be.' She would have said something more, something a great deal more enthusiastic, but there didn't seem to be any words to express what she was feeling.

William drove on in silence, only speaking again when he told her they were approaching their destination. 'Stuart claims this spot is as near paradise as one is likely to get. He'd better be right!'

'He probably is,' she encouraged him. 'Not that it matters. It's such a lovely day that I wouldn't care if we were in the middle of Piccadilly Circus!'

He looked at her, his thoughts hidden behind a mask of indifference. 'I should,' he said.

She clasped her hands tighter together. 'Why?'

He smiled ruefully. 'Because, my Georgie Porgie, today I'm going to be very gentle with you and you're going to respond in kind. Shouting above the roar of the traffic wouldn't be conducive to the kind of atmosphere I want to achieve.' He glanced across at her. 'How does the programme appeal so far?'

'I don't mind when you're not gentle,' she blurted out. 'I l-like being with you, you see.'

'Do you, darling? I think you're more generous than I deserve, because in the past I've bruised your spirit more than a little, haven't I?'

Surprisingly, she was amused by that. 'I shall enjoy having you apply a little balm,' she told him. 'William, you fool! You know it will be just the same tomorrow when you want something from me! And I'm just as big a fool. I think I must like the masterful touch!'

'The iron hand in the velvet glove? That's all very well, love, but not without love, and not without the glove. It'll be different from now on, I promise you. I've been obtuse as far as you're concerned, but my eyes are wide open now.'

'It doesn't matter,' she said uncomfortably.

'Because you're used to being misjudged?' His foot slipped on the accelerator and they shot forward, coming to rest under a group of trees close beside one of the prettiest silver waterfalls that Georgina had ever seen. 'It's going to be different from now on!'

She didn't know what to say to that. She was glad to be able to busy herself helping to spread the rug on the ground just short of the spray from the waterfall, and to carry the packages of food and drink from the jeep to the rug.

'Oh, do look!' she whispered, awed. 'That bird, over there!'

He glanced where she was pointing. 'A blue-tailed bee-eater.'

'And that?'

'A blackheaded oriole. It has a pretty mustard-coloured body which you can see better in flight. That one over there is a kingfisher.'

'But it's quite black and dull,' she complained.

'Wait until it takes off. See it?'

It flew across the water in a blaze of greeny-blue, settling on the other side of the water, its right-angled beak turning busily from side to side as the bird inspected the possibilities of his territory.

Georgina turned impulsively to William. 'Thank you for bringing me here! You looked so tired last night, and then to get up as early as you did—it was kind of you, because I didn't think I'd see you before this evening.'

'And that mattered to you?'

She nodded, embarrassed. 'It was nice having a whole week together before you started work. It spoilt me for having to entertain myself, I expect. I've never had nothing in particular to do before.'

'Enjoy it while you can,' he advised her. 'You'll be busy enough when the children make their appearance.'

'Children?' She sounded as if she had never heard the word before.

'The fruit of the marriage-bed,' he reminded her dryly.

'Oh.' She coloured and turned away, saying again, '*Oh!*'

He sat down on the rug, spreading his long legs out in front of him and patting the place beside him. 'Don't sound so surprised, Georgie. Celine seems to expect it of us, even if you don't!'

'I hadn't thought——'

'What had you thought about?'

She sat down quickly, feeling suddenly weak at the knees. 'I don't know. I was busy taking each day as it came.' She paused, gathering up her courage. 'William, about Jennifer——'

'What about her?'

'She doesn't mean half what she says. I think she is— fond of you, if that's what's worrying you.'

His eyes narrowed, the amber of his eyes looking very yellow against the black of his lashes. 'It's not. I heard all I wanted to from Jennifer last night. Not that it changed anything. You'd already wrought havoc with my feelings, long before Jennie made her appearance. You're such an innocent, Georgie! Didn't you guess how I felt?'

She bit her lip, trying not to allow the burgeoning excitement within her to get away from her rapidly diminishing control over it. 'I still don't know,' she said.

But it seemed he wasn't going to tell her—not yet. He lay back, pillowing his head on his hands, and changed the subject.

'Tell me about Jennifer,' he coaxed her. 'Tell me the truth, and make it as short as you can. She's a dull subject on such a day as this!'

'Dull?' The word exploded out of her. 'Aren't you in love with her after all? If you've changed your mind, you shouldn't have allowed her to come all this way to be with you. She'll be furious!'

'I'd say Duncan is more entitled to feel ill-used. I

wonder how she persuaded him to pay for her to visit us. It's a damned sight more than I'd do for you, Georgie! Nobody else is ever going to have you but me!'

Georgina traced the pattern of the rug with her finger, waiting for the thunder of her heart to subside a little. 'She may go back to him,' she volunteered at last. 'It's the sort of thing she would do. Perhaps he knows that. He might have been prepared to take a gamble on her, don't you think?'

'Possibly.'

'She's a bit spoilt,' Georgina continued, picking her words with care. 'Our parents have always given her her own way——'

'*And so have you!*'

'She's younger than I am. I could always look after myself, but she's such a delicate little thing——'

'So I thought too! But not for long. I soon discovered which one of you needed protecting from the wolves of this world—*and it wasn't her*!'

Georgina looked at him then. 'You mean me?' she asked, astonished.

He smiled slowly at her puzzled expression. 'I daresay you'd manage well enough in a fair fight,' he consoled her, 'but wolves in sheep's clothing seldom fight fair. Like Jennifer!'

She accepted that, but she wasn't going to let him get away with his own deeds so lightly. 'Do you fight fair?' she challenged him.

His eyes met hers. 'Are you lodging a complaint?'

She shook her head. 'I don't want you to think badly of Jennie, that's all.'

He propped himself up on to his elbow, unbalancing her as he did so and triumphantly imprisoning her against the long length of his body.

'Jennifer can live with my opinion of her. I doubt it will so much as dent her self-conceit. But last night was the last time she takes you apart in my hearing. There's no comparison between the two of you, and I was lucky enough to get the best of the bargain when I pushed you into marriage with me. I knew it almost at once, and I thought you knew how I felt too. I forgot women have to have everything put into words before they'll allow themselves to believe a man's fallen in love with them—and you more than most, because you still think everyone is going to prefer Jennifer to yourself, don't you? Well, it isn't true. You didn't only black my eye, my darling; you hit me hard where it hurts most, and I couldn't believe my good fortune that I'd made my bed with you and had every right to make love to you as often as I could persuade you to co-operate!'

She veiled her eyes with her long lashes. 'I love you,' she said.

He ran his fingers round the collar of her dress, finding the top of the zip. 'I know that, sweetheart.'

Her eyes opened wide. 'How could you know?'

His lips found the hollow between her breasts. 'You told me so.'

'When?' His closeness disturbed her breathing and she put up a hand to prevent his from exploring any further. 'I'm sure I didn't!'

'Not in words perhaps, but I knew. You might have known how I felt about you too, if you'd thought about it. You must have known how much I wanted you!'

'That isn't quite the same thing,' she said primly.

His eyes lit with laughter as he kissed her. 'With you, I think it is, my lovely wife. You have a rare talent for love.'

'Mmm,' she murmured, distracted by the increasing passion of his kisses. 'I've loved you ever since I was ten years old, only I wasn't going to admit it! You wouldn't have made me marry you otherwise, William Ayres! I might not have known it was love exactly, but I knew I was going to marry you as soon as you kissed me when I came to tell you about Jennifer and Duncan.'

'Hush,' he commanded her. 'You talk too much. Be quiet and let me kiss you some more!'

But, laughing a little, she wriggled away from him to the far edge of the rug, turning her back on him. 'I thought this was going to be my time,' she reminded him, her voice not quite steady. 'I thought you were going to be gentle and loving——'

He plucked a leaf and tickled the back of her neck with it. For a moment he considered hauling her back into his arms whether she would or not, but then he acknowledged the justice of her complaint.

'Okay, little Georgina, what is it you want to know?'

She turned over to face him, her expression very serious. 'I want to know when you began to love me. You didn't at first. You were much too involved with Jennifer to notice me at all.'

He bent forward and kissed the tip of her nose. 'Not nearly as involved as you thought. I was attracted, that's all, and she seemed a very suitable person to deal with Celine. *Not* my most intelligent move, I know, but fortunately you came along and with great energy put an end to that arrangement for me.' His smile deepened, but the glint in his tawny eyes had nothing to do with amusement. 'I started falling for you when you claimed you were better stacked than Jennie. You are too!'

'Oh, William, I didn't! I might have indicated that I am—well, better endowed——'

His delighted laughter effectively silenced her. 'It amounts to the same thing,' he teased her. 'Is that all you want to know?'

There had to be a hundred other questions she wanted to ask him, but she couldn't think of one of them. She edged a few inches closer to him, overcome by the gush of warm excitement she felt as his arms closed about her.

'William, please love me!' she begged him.

Shé put her hands against his chest and discovered that his heart was beating as fast as hers. 'William?' she murmured, opening her lips to the pressure of his.

'I'm waiting to do so,' he said.

# YOU'LL L♥VE
## *Harlequin Magazine*

**for women who enjoy reading fascinating stories of exciting romance in exotic places**

## SUBSCRIBE NOW!

This is a colorful magazine especially designed and published for the readers of Harlequin novels.

Now you can receive your very own copy delivered right to your home every month throughout the year for only 75¢ an issue.

This colorful magazine is available only through Harlequin Reader Service, so enter your subscription now!

# *In every issue...*

Here's what you'll find:

♥ a complete, full-length romantic novel...illustrated in color.

♥ exotic travel feature...an adventurous visit to a romantic faraway corner of the world.

♥ delightful recipes from around the world...to bring delectable new ideas to your table.

♥ reader's page...your chance to exchange news and views with other Harlequin readers.

♥ other features on a wide variety of interesting subjects.

Start enjoying your own copies of Harlequin magazine immediately by completing the subscription reservation form.

## *Not sold in stores!*